Jon's gaze touched her, lingering deliberately. "Poor Sophie. Are you really a dried flower? You've been playing the full Victorian maiden since Pierre Cascelt dumped you three years ago. Other people have let you hide your emotions away. I won't." His blue eyes gleamed with speculation. "I'd enjoy making love to you."

Jon's knowledge and his assertions swept away the floodgates of Sophie's control. He had ripped past the layers of hurt and grief.

"Get out! Get out this minute!" she shouted in anguish.

"The truth hurting?" He went to touch her, but Sophie backed off.

"I wouldn't let you touch me if you were down on your knees!"

"Groveling's not my style." He laughed.

Rosalie Henaghan, born and raised in New Zealand, was inspired to write after interviewing Harlequin Romance author Essie Summers on radio. Now Rosalie is the author of many books, whose unique quality stems from her use of events and elements from her own life to enhance her stories. She is convinced that a writer should examine her own background and then, as Essie told her, ''start writing!''

Books by Rosalie Henaghan

HARLEQUIN ROMANCE
1422—THE SOPHISTICATED URCHIN
2462—COPPERS GIRL
2572—THE MAN FROM TI KOUKA
2621—FOR EVER AND A DAY
2751—SAFE HARBOUR

Spell of
the Mountains

Rosalie Henaghan

Harlequin Books

TORONTO • NEW YORK • LONDON
AMSTERDAM • PARIS • SYDNEY • HAMBURG
STOCKHOLM • ATHENS • TOKYO • MILAN

Original hardcover edition published in 1989
by Mills & Boon Limited

ISBN 0-373-03027-4

Harlequin Romance first edition January 1990

CHAPTER ONE

BLUE eyes looking directly at her made Sophie Wilton pause in her quick flick through the glossy magazine. The man in the picture had so much vitality, he looked as if he was about to stride straight out of the photo and start giving orders.

'I wouldn't want to run across your path,' Sophie murmured. 'You look the type who only cares about getting his own way.'

The caption held her interest. 'Hotelier, man of the month,' it announced. 'In the spotlight is Jon Roberts. Well known in the New Zealand hotel trade for his luxury Auckland hotel The Kingdom (where every guest is a royal one) and in the scenic resorts of the Bay of Islands, Taupo and Rotorua for his Millionaire Motor Hotels and Lodges, Jon has set the rumours running with the prospect that he is to establish certainly one, but possibly two Kingdoms further south. Reason? Jon's spectacular tourism coup! Working with a giant North American chain, Jon has planned holidays and can already register four thousand confirmed bookings for the next season. Seems as if we all like the idea of being treated as a royal or a millionaire, for a week or two at least, and Jon Roberts and his staff are pledged to make it happen!'

Sophie's glance went back to the photo again. The man was irritatingly good-looking, she decided. Strong bone-structure gave his face an arresting quality, and she could see the aggressiveness even though the hand-tailored suit attempted to camouflage it into businesslike acceptability. Dark brown hair was swept into a trendy hairstyle clever enough to take into account its natural tendency to fall forward on to the broad forehead.

'I bet you're a real player!' Sophie muttered. 'And about as two-faced as a tennis racquet!'

Automatically she began reading the dark-print side column which accompanied the photo.

Full Name:	Jonathon Arthur Roberts
Age:	Thirty
Marital Status:	Single
Occupation:	Hotelier
Wealth:	Depends on the computer readout
Interests:	Making money
Most memorable experience:	A brunette
Biggest challenge:	A redhead
Worst mistake:	Let's just say I'm not into blondes.

Sophie glared at the man in the photo. 'You're not funny!' Her own blonde hair tumbled and danced indignantly as her brown eyes addressed the picture.

'Favourite pub: The Kindgom, of course. Wife: One day I suppose it will be inevitable. She'll have to like children. I see myself in a patriarchal mould as I age. It's just a pity that polygamy isn't a New Zealand custom.'

Sophie thumped the magazine closed. 'I haven't time to waste on you!' She felt like throwing the magazine into her rubbish bag, but it had been expensive, and there were other articles which were excellent. Carefully she replaced it on the table. She kept several magazines to provide interest for the different guests at her small motel units.

She stood back and surveyed the unit with a critical, proprietorial gaze. The cushions were set at a welcoming angle, the twin pictures of nearby Mount Hutt ski-field were straight, the basket of dried flowers she had used to replace the more usual fresh flowers and leaves of autumn looked pretty, their colours toning perfectly with the blues and peaches of the unit. She walked into the bathroom to check the spare towels, then entered the large bedroom with its giant waterbed and monitored the switch. Meticulously she straightened the smooth lie of the curtains. She frowned as she spotted the fingermark on the window—she had nearly missed it. From her overall pocket she tugged a canister and a cloth. Deftly she squirted a puff of white foam over the area, then rubbed at it until her reflection was revealed, brown eyes emphasised by the pile of long blonde hair caught high on one side to keep it off her face. The style added a couple more inches to her five-feet-five height, but also made her look younger than twenty-three.

She pulled a face at herself, then returned to studying the unit. Even someone like the hotelier in the *Spotlight* column wouldn't be able to fault it, she thought proudly. He wasn't the only one to treat his guests royally. The thought crossed her mind that, although they both had the same business, he had become a millionaire, while she was still struggling to pay back the loan her father had taken out to build the six units three years previously. Jon Roberts would organise others to do the work, to keep his hotel and lodges running; she was her own one-woman receptionist, cleaner, manageress and typist.

At least I know who to blame if anything's wrong! she thought, smiling, as she bundled the cloths and rubbish on to the trolley waiting outside the unit. She shut the door and set off down the path, pushing the trolley in front of her. Her shoulders sagged and the perky hairstyle wobbled as she admitted weariness.

She looked ahead of her at the view of the mountains and was cheered by the sight. Pleasure helped her draw in a deep breath of the fresh air. Outlined by the weathered grey fences and the deep green-black of the shelterbelts, the green, olive and brown squares and rectangles of the plains led to the shocking vertical immensity of the giant ranges of mountain peaks serrating and slashing the sky. Snow, the first fall of winter, had coated the tops and reached white-gloved fingers towards the lower bush slopes.

A small stone caught the trolley's wheel and she stumbled as it jarred against her foot. The savage, unexpected pain brought her attention back to the path in front of her. So much for lifting her eyes to the hills!

The wide sweep of lawn reminded her of yet another task which needed her attention. It was all very well living in a house with a garden setting if the income to supply gardener and housekeeper was available, but otherwise . . . She pushed the trolley to the rear of the large, colonial homestead. A big utility-room had been made from one of the old store-rooms and Sophie deftly unpacked the trolley.

Fifteen minutes later, rejuvenated by a shower, she walked into the kitchen. Her father, Theo Wilton, was in the act of pouring cups of tea.

'You'll be as dry as a paddock in February, I'm thinking.' He passed her a drink.

'Thanks, Dad. It seemed to take me ages to do everything today. We had total occupancy last night. Pulled the bank balance up wonderfully.' Her brown eyes shone. 'Pity the local golf club doesn't hold tournaments more often. I wonder how their games went.'

'It's a long time since you took time off to play. Sometimes I think the worst thing I ever did was to let you talk me into building the units. You work far too hard.'

'Won't make the body-building champs this year,' Sophie smiled. She pulled her hand back to her shoulder in a mock muscle-exercise. 'I'm fine, Dad. Oh, of course I get fed up with cleaning sometimes, but I really enjoy seeing the units look just right. And people do appreciate it. So many of our clients come out of their way to stay here because someone else has told them about us.'

'The best motor hotel units in the South Island,' her father teased.

'Well, I think they are,' Sophie countered. 'I just wish there was some way to fill them all year round. In winter and early spring I could fill them ten times over with the ski season, but after that it's just a trickle.'

'People are mad. Summer is the best time in Methven. We've got more than just mountains. There are the lakes and the rivers; fishing, boating and peace and quiet. Promotion is what you should consider, Sophie.'

'You're probably right. But I've been putting every cent back into repayment of the loan. The interest rate is so high.'

'I must admit our solicitor was impressed with the rate you're repaying the capital. Maybe you should start taking a proper salary.'

'I'd rather get the loan down. Once that's lower we could afford to have advertising and possibly I could hire extra help part-time.'

'Well, it's your pigeon, Sophie. I'll stick to my farming.' He pulled his woolly hat on to his sandy-covered scalp as he stood up. Moments later, Sophie heard his tuneless whistle as he walked towards the fence he had been repairing. She put the dishes into the dishwasher and began the preparations for the evening meal. Finished, she checked the clock and decided she had time to run down to the village to buy stamps and get some fresh fruit. The previous night's full occupancy could be reason to celebrate. She slung on her backpack, fetched her purse and shut the office door after putting the 'Back in five minutes' sign into position.

The day was the crystal brightness of early winter. Beside her, the Southern Alps were a giant backdrop to the stage of the Canterbury Plains. The Mount Hutt ski field road looked like a thread of unravelled black wool a child had dropped on a still wet canvas. Sophie slowed from her easy jog to a walk as she turned the corner to see the group of shops. Outside the post office she recognised her neighbour and childhood friend, Harry Southton. He was like the brother she had always wanted.

'Just the person I hoped to see. I'm playing Lady Bountiful, taking pity on your solitary status and inviting you to partake of a meal tonight.' Sophie chuckled. 'In other words, we're having a roast dinner and it'll be cold meat all week if you don't come!'

'How can I refuse?' Harry's brown eyes twinkled down at her from his six feet. 'What about a movie afterwards?'

'Not tonight, Harry. Dad's got a meeting and . . .'

'You can't leave the units,' he finished with parrot-like practice. 'Come and have a drink now.' He gestured to the popular pub at the crossroads.

'No, thanks, I've . . .'

'Got to get back to work.' He smiled. 'Take time to breathe, won't you?'

She waved goodbye as she went into the post office and bought the sheet of stamps she required. One of her friends was in the dairy and she stopped to chat, for once forgetful of the passing minutes. Guilt pressed on her heels, the pack thumping uncomfortably on her back as she ran towards her home.

Tiromaunga was one of the area's oldest homesteads. Originally built by Sophie's great-grandparents, it had begun life in considerable style, reflecting the prosperity they had found in the new land. Their family of fifteen, twelve of whom had survived infancy, had necessitated a large dwelling and gardens to match. Sophie's great-grandmother had been primarily responsible for the import of trees from around the globe, and her two gardeners had established a tree-lined drive and a large orchard protected by parklike groupings of trees surrounding the homestead. A hundred years later, each autumn the trees were magnificent fires of colour: red, yellow, gold, orange, scarlet and brown mingling with the groups of natives and conifers. Because of the screen of trees the homestead had almost complete privacy, but the motel units on the opposite side of the driveway could be seen through the old pine shelterbelt at the road.

As she ran down the driveway Sophie noted automatically the last dying colours, the skeletal outlines of the trees, and the thickness of the leaf carpet under the trees. The drive split, one side to lead to the units, the other to the homestead. At the fork, parked neatly, was a low-slung, high-powered vehicle. Sophie had learnt a great deal of different makes and models since running the motel, but this was a car such as she had only seen in glossy, up-market magazines.

She slowed, looking around for the owner. No one

appeared. She frowned, hoping the potential customer had not been too annoyed by her lengthy 'five minutes'.

The car was immediately in front of her, and its sleek appeal was impossible to ignore. Carefully she ran her hand over the gleaming bonnet. It was still warm, which told her the car had come some distance, and had only just been switched off.

'Superb body.' The man's voice was rich and full of laughter.

Sophie spun, feeling almost gauche, knowing the owner had seen her action. His lightning approving glance left her in no doubt as to whose body he was referring. He had been camouflaged by the trees, with his dark brown hair, tanned face, brown leather jacket and dark trousers.

Six feet of hard-packed muscle on bone walked towards her with an athlete's lightness. It was almost a shock to see that the man had blue eyes, the dazzling blue of a mountain tarn.

'You must be Sophie Wilton.' He smiled again, and she felt a flicker of immediate response being drawn from her despite her instinctive wariness. The man was just too good-looking, and there was a familiarity somewhere. Rapidly she searched the computer banks of her memory. He was a man who would not be forgotten easily, but the screen of her thoughts remained blank.

'That's correct. Welcome to Tiromaunga. I'm sorry. You seem to have the advantage of me. I can't recall meeting you before.'

'We haven't met. My name's Jon Roberts. Friends

told me about you. They didn't exaggerate. You look like a daffodil of spring in this setting.'

'Yellow and green spikes,' Sophie smiled.

'You're right. Not a daffodil, perhaps an Earlicheer narcissus, pale creamy flowers. Just the colour of your hair.'

Sophie studied the man while she smiled. 'Thank you. I'm sure you didn't drive here just to make pretty compliments. Were you looking for accommodation?'

'Yes, I'd like a unit for the night. Just a single will be OK.'

'Turn here and you'll come to number six. It's the one with the turret on this end. I'll just drop these things off home and pick up the keys. If it's unsuitable, you can tell me then and there.'

'Sounds fine.'

Aware of his scrutiny, she was glad when the curve of the homestead driveway hid her from his view. She was strangely unsettled; the man had so much charm and such good looks. She reached the homestead, dumped the backpack and took a small bottle of milk from the refrigerator. On the way out she picked up her set of keys as well as the keys to unit six.

The sleek sports car was parked neatly outside the unit, and a suitcase stood by the door. The man himself was standing further back, studying the layout. He turned to her.

'Your architect deserves his award. His use of wood and stone is so right in this setting. I like his steeply pitched roofline and the turrets at each end;

it fits with the homestead and with the mountains.'

Sophie was impressed. Few ever commented on just why the buildings were so pleasing to the eye. The man was perceptive.

'Are you an architect yourself?'

'No, though I'll admit I've had considerable work with them. David Alfield was the architect here, wasn't he?'

'Yes, do you know him?'

'Not yet. I think I'll make a point of meeting him soon. What's he like?'

'He has an office in Christchurch, but his parents live only two miles down the road. David practically grew up here. His parents and mine were best friends. The Alfields were very helpful when my mother was sick, and after she died they were very supportive. Dad and I think the world of them.' She realised she had digressed into personal details. 'Sorry, I don't normally bore people with my history.'

His eyes were the reflection of understanding. 'So naturally, when you were considering the options, you asked David Alfield.'

Sophie nodded. 'Actually, it was partly his idea originally. He understood that I wanted to stay at home, but our farm isn't big enough to support two incomes, so he suggested using the homestead as a bed and breakfast inn.' She smiled, remembering the explosion that suggestion had caused from her father. 'Let's just say Dad didn't agree. That's when we thought of building. But don't get me on to my hobby horse. I love my units.'

'I really am very interested. Look, you've milk there. Spare me a few minutes and have a cup of coffee with me. I'm sure your units have kettles and cups.' His smile dazzled her and she found herself nodding. She wanted to see his reaction to the interior.

She stood aside as he entered, allowing him to get the impact of the superb view across the paddocks to the massive mountains. He studied the view for a moment, then surveyed the room, walking up the two small steps to the turret hexagonal window to get the advantage of several angles.

'Magnificent!' He walked back across the room to the bedroom, dumped his suitcase and Sophie heard him stride through to check the bathroom and the kitchen. The sound of the kettle being filled reminded her of the milk in her hand.

'Congratulations! This unit is world class. Quite superb! I think this is one of the few times I've walked into a strange motel or hotel and felt immediately welcomed and at ease.' He plugged in the kettle. 'Coffee coming up. Your interior designer was very sensitive to the architect. The textures and the colours are restful and subtly pleasing. Quite different from the usual stereotype unit. Who was the designer?'

Sophie took a bow.

'You?' He looked surprised. 'Did you study interior design?'

'No. Possibly one day . . .' She pointed to a tin. 'There are some biscuits there.'

'Better and better. Home-made. Yours, too?'

'Yes,' admitted Sophie. 'I don't bake in the ski season, I'm just too busy. But this is our quiet time.'

'I'm surprised you're not hanging out the "No vacancy" sign every night.'

'Wish we were! We do have a lot of repeat business, but we're too small to catch the tour operators. We haven't the capacity for a busload of tourists, unfortunately.'

'Why don't you extend? I noticed the mains and the sewer running along the front of the roadside.'

'A flush of enthusiasm from the local council after we gained our zoning change!'

His expression told her he enjoyed the witticism. She began to relax. It was so pleasant to get such sincere and clearly knowledgeable compliments.

'David's original idea was for ten units. Dad insisted six was the maximum. Apart from the capital involved, he didn't really want to lose the land. He needs more land for the farm, not less.'

'But surely he could buy a few acres from someone else round here? Hotel/motel-zoned land is far too valuable to just have an odd sheep grazing on it.'

She finished her coffee and nodded agreement. 'Dad tried for a long time. We have the town boundary on one side and on the other is Harry Southton's place. His farm is even smaller, so he's not able to sell any land. Across the road is reserve land. Ironically, it was given to the county by my great-grandfather to preserve the beauty of the view. That's where the name Tiromaunga comes from.'

'Sight of the mountains?' Jon queried.

'That's right.' Sophie pulled herself up. 'Sorry, I

didn't mean to talk about the units. I did warn you!'
The man was just too attractive and charming. She
had to break the golden ribbon of attraction which
had been tied so easily. She looked down at the set of
keys. 'Excuse me, I'll have to go to close the
windows on the others.'

'Allow me to escort you. I'd like to see them.'

Sophie was taken aback, but there was no reason
to refuse. 'If you're interested.'

He followed as she led the way along the concrete
walkway. She was very conscious of him as he stood
beside her when she unlocked the next unit's door. A
faint, pleasing aroma from his aftershave impinged
on her consciousness. Briskly she walked inside and
went to the kitchen, bedroom and bathroom to close
the windows. On her return, Jon had shut the
lounge ones and he stood observing the unit. They
repeated the process through the remainder.

As they returned to unit six his quietness worried
her. She reminded herself she knew nothing about
the man. Good looks could be a trap. His quietness
gave her a reason for speaking.

'Is there something wrong?' Sophie hesitated in
her question.

'No. I'm just thinking. You have a real talent for
interior design. Each unit is quite a definite entity,
yet most furniture and furnishings would mix and
match well. That's a good practical design. The
middle one is the only one I felt you had left a little
bare. Was there a reason?'

'Yes. We had a Japanese foreign exchange student
living with us for a year when I was at high school.

Their rooms are quite different. That unit can convert to a *ryoken* style very easily. When we have the occasional Japanese visitors I try to give them that one. They always feel very comfortable there.'

'Can you speak Japanese?'

'I couldn't help but pick up a little!'

'Handy. Any other languages?'

'My French is better. We had a marvellous teacher at school and I had . . .' she broke off, then recovered '. . . a friend who spoke French.'

She moved to his bedroom to turn down the sheets. The movement gave her a chance to examine herself. What was she doing, telling the man all her story? It was almost as if he had been pumping her for information, she realised. She had been burbling on, telling all about her parents, her friends and the units, yet she knew nothing of him. Why had he been so interested? Wasn't it just a little strange? But, what did it matter? At the doorway she paused, confident that her manner was poised.

'The office is in the homestead. You can pay by cash, credit card or cheque. If there is anything else you want, just ask. If I can help, I will.'

The blue in his eyes deepened as his face crinkled into a knowing smile, and Sophie silently cursed her choice of phrase. His mouth opened for a soft chuckle, revealing strong white teeth. She wanted to laugh with him but decided it would be giving him too much leeway. Her breath caught in her throat as his gaze on her changed at her expression. Although he was not physically touching her, it felt as if he was running his hands over her body, intimately touching, holding and stroking. With exquisite slowness he was making love to her with his eyes. A tiny muscle in her lip quivered as though under attack.

'Have you quite finished?' she snapped tightly.

'You did ask for it,' he replied casually. 'You're an attractive woman, Sophie. I just had to see if I wanted you, too. If you're interested, I've decided in your favour.'

'That's not funny.'

He stood and suddenly he was crisp and authoritative. 'You misunderstand. But I'll come back to that later. I'd rather deal with the main subject first. I want to buy the units.'

A shaft of sunlight tipped the brown curls with light and his blue eyes studied her. He looked just like the man in the *Spotlight* photograph. The man of the month, hotelier Jon . . . Jonathon Roberts. She felt suddenly like an open-mouthed salmon that had propelled out of the water on to rocks. She gasped for air.

'Did you say you wanted to buy the units?' Surprise, shock and anger warred.

'That's right.'

'But they're not for sale.' She struggled against her anger with him. 'I've just realised who you are. Don't you feel a little honesty on your part would have been better?'

'I told you my name. If you don't bother to keep yourself informed, that's your problem. I found it quite interesting to see just how you welcome your guests. I've already given you my opinion on the lodge. Now, all that remains is to negotiate a price.'

'You're overlooking the major point. The units are not on the market.'

'A minor point.'

'That's where we disagree. My father has no intention of selling.' Sophie was annoyed by his persistence.

'Everything has its price.'

'In your world, perhaps.'

'Don't be a self-righteous prig.' At her gasp of indignation a glimmer of a smile showed. 'Just a passing observation.'

Sophie felt her eyes widen. Just who did Jon Roberts think he was? He might be a king in his own castle, but he certainly wasn't the ruler in hers! To think she had felt the man was attractive!

'The lodge legally belongs to your father. Your name is not mentioned on the deeds. However, according to my research, they were built because of you and for you. If you told your father to sell, he'd sell them immediately. He never has liked the idea of you running the units, and he doesn't approve of the hours you spend looking after them.'

'How do you know?' Outrage flashed in her brown eyes.

'I pay to know the facts. I'm a businessman.'

'You mean you had spies here? Checking on us?'

'If you want to use that childish terminology. I had a feasibility study made.'

'You—what?'

'I used the services of professionals. A retired building inspector, an engineer and a physchologist to investigate the possibilities. Before that I had land agents who did most of the preliminary work. Their assessments are all studied. In your case it was simple. They were among your guests here. They had the on-the-spot chance to study the details, and you and your father. Anything they didn't know, the folk around about willingly supplied.'

'You, you . . .!'

'Just listen. I know it's a shock, but after a while you'll be able to think rationally.'

'I am rational!' Indignation steamed in her voice. 'I repeat: the units are not for sale.'

'You're supposed to be intelligent.'

'And being intelligent means I cave in and see things your way! Why should I sell?' She realised too late that she had already shifted her fortress to a less defensive position with her question.

'One reason is money. Another is the good it would do the community; I intend to build a large complex. It will give permanent employment for many local people on a year-round basis. On a personal level, your father could afford to have improvements made on the farm and the homestead. He could have a couple of overseas trips, have some leisure in his life.'

The thought of it was tempting. Her father did deserve a break. He worked so hard. She only just caught the quick gleam in his blue eyes. He thought she was hooked. No doubt the psychologist had told him to use her love as a weapon.

'You can still build elsewhere in the area.'

'True. I'm sure I'd have immediate support from the local council. I ordered reports on three other possibilities. The facts remain that your site is the best. The size of the property will allow me to develop just what I want. The others are limiting.'

'With all your experts, I'm sure you could overcome them.' Her tone was scathing.

'Even I can't shift a mountain. This is the best site. I'd buy the units and eighteen acres plus the front paddock to the road.'

She knew his admission was meant to disarm her. His smile was so natural. If she wasn't so shocked and angry about his spying on her she could have found herself responding.

'I've tried to see it your way, Sophie. You've regarded the lodge as your pet project from the beginning. But you've had a struggle. You didn't know the first thing about running units and the capital required. There's more to it than making beds! You've managed very well because you've been prepared to work and be on call from early morning till late at night.'

'Don't patronise me!' Sophie was incensed by his logic.

He moved towards her, his blue eyes bright gleams of speculation. 'It's been all hard work and no play for you, Sophie. Don't you know you're a woman?'

His gaze touched her, lingering deliberately on her mouth. It was like a physical bruising. His touch on her hair lifting the thick coil of hair off her face, his hand stroking the side of her face in a caress was sensual intimacy. She forced herself to look away, not admitting the surge which had coursed through her at his actual warmth on her skin.

'Don't touch me!'

'Poor Sophie. Are you really a dried flower?' He broke off one of the dried flowers from the basket on the shelf. 'The shape, the exquisite colour, even a trace of the perfume is still there,' he murmured. 'The flower is the sex organ of the plant. Dried, it's useless.'

Sophie felt his glance strip away all her pretence, ripping past the layers of hurt and grief unshed. Her only protection was her anger with him against the sudden vulnerability.

'How dare you?'

'Well, you've been playing the full Victorian maiden since Pierre Cascelt dumped you three years ago. Your father and Harry Southton have let you hide your emotions away. I won't. I'd enjoy making love to you.' His knowledge and his assertions swept away the floodgates of her control.

'Get out! Get out this minute!'

'The truth hurting?' He went to touch her, but Sophie backed off.

'I wouldn't let you touch me if you were down on your knees.'

'Grovelling's not my style.' He laughed. His urbanity and control angered Sophie to white heat.

'Go! Go right now! I don't even want you staying here. You can sleep in a ditch for all I care. Maybe an irrigation one. Cold water might do you some good.'

Anger torched the blue eyes so briefly that Sophie thought she'd imagined it. He turned and walked into the bedroom and stood by his suitcase.

'How are you going to throw me out?' He asked the question as if it were academic. She was almost disappointed she hadn't pierced his imperturbability. The man was a robot!

'Well?'

His taunt made Sophie's temper rise again. She had said the words, but she would look ridiculous if she attempted to push him herself. Without some form of enforcement the words were another source of mockery. Eventually her father would come, but to wait for him would be a humiliating defeat. She couldn't hand Jon Roberts such a victory!

CHAPTER TWO

'COME on! Evict me!'

Deliberately Jon Roberts changed his stance, folding his arms. He looked invincible. Sophie gritted her teeth so her tormentor wouldn't know just how desperate she felt. The sight of the old bull grazing contentedly in the paddock outside gave her inspiration. With serene poise, she walked to the door.

'All I have to do is walk out and open one gate.' She saw the question in his eyes. 'The bull would charge. No, not you, Mr Roberts, he's harmless with people. Just your car. This was his old territory, and he's never forgiven the cars which drove him out. Let's just say your machine would be a panelbeater's joy . . .' She let the words hang and opened the door of the unit.

'Ingenious! You fight well, Sophie.' He picked up his suitcase and walked towards the triumphantly held door. 'For that I'll give you a warning. The units will be mine before your birthday. As for you . . .'

Sophie had been so dazzled by her victory that she didn't realise Jon Roberts had invaded her space. Almost leisurely, he put down his suitcase and jacket and surveyed her. When she began to move, his arms shot out on either side so that his hands were almost touching her waist, trapping her against the surface of the door. He moved so that they were only a few inches apart, his blue eyes challenging. The smell of his aftershave was subtle, adding to the mix of Sophie's emotions of dismay, doubt, fear, anger and physical attraction. His apparent calmness gave her the answer. Jon Roberts was used to keeping his own feelings under a steel coat. She would have to learn how to wear a similar garment.

'What do you think you're doing?' Her voice held the snow of the mountains.

'Is it so long since a man kissed you?'

'I thought you'd already decided I was a dried flower.'

'Given evidence, I could change my mind.'

Sophie saw his glance travel appraisingly to her mouth and she willed herself to appear still, tightening her fingers into stiffly held fists, to control her feelings. Not until he was stopped by her silence and looked back at her eyes did she answer.

'Your opinion of me is irrelevant.' Scornfully she let her gaze cover him from head to toe in the same appraising manner. 'My opinion of *you* . . . it's so low that I'd find it easier to kiss a snake.'

Jon's blue eyes flashed anger, but his eyelids hooded almost immediately. Sophie wished she hadn't uttered her last phrase.

'Not my greatest compliment,' Jon Roberts spoke quietly, but he had moved back and picked up his jacket and suitcase.

Relieved, Sophie unclenched her balled fists and

moved away from the door.

'Let's have a small wager, Sophie. You say I won't buy the lodge. I'm telling you I will. I'll even give you a time limit. Before your birthday? If I win, you will either kiss a snake or . . .' his smile held irony '. . . kiss me.'

'You . . . You won't win! But if by my birthday you haven't bought the units, then you have to promise to leave us alone in the future. No attempting to buy up our business later?'

'A woman after my own heart! Always business! It's a bet.' He ran down the steps to his car. Moments later Sophie heard the roar of its motor echoing along the drive. Only then did she move slowly, like a frail invalid, to the comfort of the sofa. She had won! Her emotions were whirling faster than spinning tops, but she had won! Her birthday was less than three months away. In that time Jon Roberts would not be able to persuade her father to sell. She smiled, remembering how long it had taken her to persuade him to build them in the first place.

Jon Roberts and his commercial world held no menace for the quiet, slow thoughtfulness of men like her father. She looked out of the window. The calm majesty of the mountains was solid, reassuring, protective. Just viewing the peaceful scene made her feel less threatened. The lugubrious bellow of the bull broke into her thoughts and she smiled, remembering her moment of inspiration. She owed the bull an extra tickle. Jon Roberts didn't need to know that the bull was about as ferocious as a Persian kitten!

Her smile died as she realised that Jon Roberts had not become a millionaire by pussyfooting past people's emotions. He had let her snare herself, charmingly asking her questions, leading her on until he had her convinced of his pleasant friendship, then with stunning swiftness he had struck, telling her of his intention to own the lodge. When she'd resisted he had dropped his blows deliberately, callously. Caught, she had all too easily lost her temper and placed herself in an invidious position. His comparison with the dried flower still stung. She turned and walked slowly across the room, stooping to pick up the broken flower where it had fallen. Gently she placed it in her pocket.

She wasn't a dried flower. Physically she had been attracted to him, but that was something else Jon Roberts need never know!

Sophie had barely crossed back to the homestead and repaired her appearance when the office bell pealed. Her heart began thudding as she wondered if Jon Roberts had reappeared. Reason and a glance out of the window reassured her. The pleasant, ordinary family who waited were soon settled and Sophie checked her books to verify the arrival time of one of her regular clients.

Her father was in the kitchen when she returned. He looked so tired that Sophie could not burden him with the anxieties and details of the afternoon.

'Wish I didn't have to go to the area council meeting tonight,' he muttered.

'Have a rest and a shower for half an hour while I get busy with the vegetables. I invited Harry for dinner, too. He'll be here soon.'

'Good thinking. I hate going out and leaving you to cope on your own.'

'That wasn't the reason I invited Harry! I'm quite capable.' She dusted off some flour from her hands as though she were a prize fighter.

'All the better! You do know I'd be a very happy man if you married Harry.'

'Marry Harry?' The sound made her chuckle. 'Dad, Harry's just a very dear friend!'

'Best place to start. Your mother and I had known each other all our lives.'

'Dad, you and Mum fell in love. There's a difference,' she protested.

'Sometimes I think there's a case for arranged marriages.' Her father ignored her previous statement. 'You're an only child, so one day you'll inherit the farm and Tiromaunga. Running the farm is not your choice, and you've already got the lodge and the homestead to keep you busy. But Tiromaunga is an old place, and it costs a lot to maintain. Next door there's Harry Southton. He's your age, strong as a shire horse, and making the best of a farm that, like ours, is just too small to be economic. Now, if you married, the two farms would really be a great unit.'

'I'm glad you're only theorising, Dad. Don't tell me it's time I settled down and started giving you grandchildren!'

'Well, you're not sixteen. You'll be twenty-four in a couple of months' time. Harry's a good man, Sophie. He's a man you can trust. Not one of these fly-by-night characters. Harry's solid rock.'

'Maybe that's his trouble, Dad.' Sophie managed a smile. 'I do understand, Dad, but there's as much romance between Harry and I as between a wet beach towel and a bucket of sand. We go together, but that's it. I'm useful as a partner for him and vice versa. I invited him over tonight simply because I know he loves a roast dinner and on his own it's not practical.'

Her father's snort was emphasised as he pushed his chair back and it squeaked a protest on the floor. Sophie turned back to her cooking, but her eyes were bleak. She wanted to get married, she wanted to be able to give and receive love, to cherish and to be cherished. Just over three years earlier she had thought Pierre Cascelt was the ideal man. A ski instructor from the Swiss Alps, he had swept into Sophie's life like an avalanche. For a whole season they had managed to spend a lot of time together. Sophie had always loved the ski slopes, and when Pierre's duties allowed they would explore new slopes, delighting in simply being together. As the months passed Sophie had gathered the tiny pearls of knowledge about Pierre, his family and his home in Switzerland. One day they would be her family. With Pierre, everything was completely simple and simply complete.

But he had left, without warning and without explanation. Sophie had been stunned. A few days later his boss had told an anxious Sophie that Pierre had flown back to Switzerland as his wife had been in an accident. The shock had stripped Sophie like a poplar tree in the first autumn gale. She had not been able to accept that she had imagined the love they had shared. Pierre had been so tender, so charming, so thoughtful; he had told her he loved her. She was positive there had been a mistake. He was not married. Perhaps he had tried to contact her from the airport. There would be a letter, a phone call . . . Ten thousand excuses later she had realised the truth. He had just left her. No word had ever arrived.

Friends' comments about 'other fish in the sea', meant to be kind, had seared with their insensitivity. She had given her love, her whole trust to Pierre. Gradually the days had passed, helping her father on the farm, doing the gardens, cooking and cleaning the homestead. She seemed incapable of any more; shattered.

It had been David Alfield who had forced her to face up to the budgetary need to supply her own living. He had suggested running Tiromaunga as a bed and breakfast house. She had liked the idea from the beginning. It had been a blow when her father had refused. Somewhere she had suggested the units. David had been happy to sketch out plans. Her father had reluctantly agreed to view more detailed drawings.

Sophie forced her mind to probe the grey agony further. With new insight she knew her father had agreed to build simply because he had been concerned for her. The proposal had lit a spark of joy in her, and he had seen that and been unable to again dissuade her. Somehow he had found the

money, raising a hefty loan. At the start, the
financial side had never concerned her. That had
only come when realisation of the interest had hit
home and when the charges had been raised after the
first instalment. She had cut back on the expenses to
change the balance. Work had been a safety-valve
for her emotions, providing her with an immediate
excuse for avoiding invitations. It hadn't been
difficult, she hadn't felt the slightest flutter of
interest in any of the young men. Pierre had
numbed her feelings.

Until she had met Jonathon Roberts!

She pulled out the broken flower from her pocket
and set it on the window-ledge. Time had healed
her; Jon Roberts had simply ripped away the
unnecessary bandages. She had no intention of
letting someone like Jon entangle her emotionally. A
man like Harry would be gentle and considerate . . .
perhaps now she felt alive again she could fall in love
with Harry?

The barking of the dogs told her someone had
come through the rear yard. She watched from the
kitchen window as Harry walked along the path. He
was a good man, she reflected, handsome in a
rugged, outdoors way. A man who could always
provide a warm fire on a cold night.

He spotted her, and his face creased into a smile.
'Something smells good,' he announced, as he
walked into the kitchen. 'You know what they say
about the way to a man's heart.' His grin was dear,
familiar. 'Can I do anything to help?'

'I haven't quite finished setting the table, Harry.'

'No trouble.' He moved to the sideboard to help.

The lodge bell rang just as they were about to start their meal. Her father and Harry both waved her off with wicked grins, promising to leave her just a scrap of bone. On her return she rescued her dinner from the oven. The curled edges took away her appetite.

'Great dinner!' Harry teased. 'At least it was. You'll have to buy yourself a microwave for Christmas.'

'That's a good idea,' Sophie admitted. 'Once I get the capital of the loan down a little more. If only the interest charges hadn't gone up again last time. I would have felt a little less constrained.'

'You've done very well, lass,' her father reminded her. 'I won't be late tonight. The area council meetings usually run to time. I'll see you later.'

After her father had left, Harry began to help her clear away. The lodge bell summoned her yet again and she excused herself apologetically.

The memory of the man she had already thrown out made her stiffen. Forcing herself to relax, she walked down the corridor to the office at the end of the west wing. She still had to tell her father about the incident, but dinner-time hadn't been the right occasion.

Everything would be all right, she told herself; Jon Roberts would give up and build elsewhere in the village. She slowed, wondering how the prospect of such competition would affect her own lodge. Fear struck her again. How could she keep up the repayments if her trade disappeared? She was fairly hopeful that most of her regulars would continue, and in the ski season there were always people anxious for accommodation, but that alone would not give her enough . . .

The regular client was settled quickly and she returned to the homestead with the shadows of the trees flickering like worries across her path.

'What's up, Sophie?'

'Sometimes, Harry, you're just a little too perceptive.' With insight she studied him, slowly becoming aware of his real feelings, his brown eyes giving away his long-held secret.

'I love you,' he said simply.

'Oh, Harry, I had no idea.' She ran her hand through her curls in agonised disbelief.

'I know. I just hoped that one day you'd . . .'

'Fall in love with you?'

'Yes.'

Sophie looked at him. 'I wish I had. You're the kindest man I know.'

Harry bent to kiss her. His mouth was feather-light, gentle and loving. She answered him, but then broke away. It wasn't fair to let Harry go on hoping. 'I'm really sorry, Harry.'

He caressed her hair and she had a flashback to the afternoon when Jon Roberts had done the same thing. Then her feelings had been in a tornado; with Harry there wasn't even a gentle breeze.

'Harry, there are so many women who would love you. We have to stop going about together. I've leaned on you too long. I can stand on my own two feet now.'

Harry tried to smile. 'I've loved you quietly for so many years, it's strange to have it out in the open. But perhaps it's better to be a realist. I've been kidding myself, while you've been in a dream world. I'll always be your friend.'

'Thank you, Harry.'

Sophie stood quietly as Harry let himself out of the door. The dark of the night hid him after a few seconds. She felt bereft, aware of how much warmth and affection had gone from her life. How could she have worn blinkers for so long?

The chiming of the grandfather clock in the front hall recalled her to the time. She was just about out of biscuits for the units, and she couldn't sit and worry about Harry.

She needed to talk to her father. Jon Roberts would not be a man to waste time. He had warned her he would buy the lodge; she had to make sure her father was in no doubt about her feelings on the subject.

The smells of ginger and butter and golden syrup were still mingling in the kitchen from her third batch of biscuits when the sound of her father's car told her he was home. She switched the jug on to boil again.

'You still up, Sophie? Marvellous meeting! I enjoyed it. There was a well-prepared case for a salmon farm further down the river, and that set off the biggest ding-dong I've seen for an age.' He grinned reminiscently. 'Never ceases to amaze me. People say they want a decent life-style and work for their teenagers in the neighbourhood, but no one wants to pay for it or set it up or risk losing a little bit of their own. As soon as someone puts up an imaginative idea, everybody else is protesting. With a lot of them their so-called good for the community is a lot of self-protecting hot air.'

'No one suggested a big holiday resort in the neighbourhood?' Sophie raised the issue deliberately, as she poured some mugs of cocoa.

'That's an idea. You're thinking of a real scheme—hotel, restaurants, pools, adventure trips and so on? Come to think of it, that's exactly what the area could provide. That would solve the employment problem, and there's plenty of mountains and rivers for thousands to enjoy.' He paused to think. 'The site could be a problem; you'd want a fair amount of land, and something so big could swamp the whole village if you built right in the centre. It would be best on the outskirts of the village belt.'

'What about the paddock where the units are?'

'Ideal. Yes, but I need that for the farm. It was bad enough parting with the land for the units.'

Sophie chuckled gently, and her father laughed too.

'You set me up!' he protested.

'So you won't sell?'

'Don't be silly! You know I need every acre of land to farm. I'm always struggling for a few more acres. Besides, the units are your livelihood. I'm lucky to have you here. You're a daughter in a million, Sophie.'

Sophie gave her father a hug. 'There is something else you should know. I turned down an offer for the units today.'

'Someone wanted to buy the lodge? But it's not for sale.'

'And the paddock. And another eighteen acres as well.'

'You told them "No Sale"? I'm not parting with any land.'

'Yes.'

'Well, that's the end of it.'

'I doubt it! The buyer was Jonathon Roberts. He's a determined man. He'll talk to you. The title is in your name. He's already checked us out. Do you know he's had spies here? I was so angry I threw him out.' She saw the amazed look on her father's face and chuckled. 'Not physically. I threatened his car with the bull! You should have seen his car, Dad. It doesn't exactly wear an engagement ring on the bumper, but I'd say he really loves that machine! He wasn't prepared to take a risk with it, in any case.'

'Are you sure he's going to come back?'

'Quite sure. He'll hire a bulldozer if necessary!'

'He obviously made quite an impression. But it doesn't mean he's got money.'

'He owns a hotel in Auckland and several motor holiday lodges in scenic spots. All of them would be in the top class category. I read about him in one of my magazines.'

'Indeed? Then he does have the experience necessary to build a complex here. Don't worry,

Sophie, I won't sell him our land, but I know a spot that might suit.'

'Forgive me if I don't share your enthusiasm. If he builds here our lodge would have difficulty getting clients. What about our repayments?'

'No problem! All the promotion this man will do for his place will bring extra tourists.'

Sophie pulled the last tray of biscuits from the oven, feeling better, her little world tidy, well-ordered. Her units were safe from Jon Roberts. And so was she!

'Dad, I'm going into Ashburton this afternoon. Do you need anything there?'

'Yes, I've been waiting for the replacement pump. Pick it up for me, will you, at the engineers? It should have been ready last week.'

Sophie added the request to her shopping list. 'You'll be around the homestead to check calls, won't you, Dad?'

'Yes. Don't worry, I'll look out for a tycoon driving a bulldozer!'

She laughed as she headed to the garage to drive out her own vehicle. The trip to the nearest town held lots of interest to a farmer's daughter, and Sophie still helped her father often enough to be familiar with all the everyday tasks on the land. She waved to one farmer and tooted to another on his tractor, debated briefly if she had time to visit friends on the way, then decided to call on her return, and shortly afterwards she was driving down the central street of Ashburton. She turned into the side street for the engineers first.

'The pump's just about finished, Miss Wilton. Can you pop back later on?'

'I'll make it an hour.' Sophie glanced at her watch. It would take her that length of time to get her own shopping. She had ordered the supplies for the units, but they would have to be checked, and she had hoped for a few minutes' browsing in the fashion shop.

An hour later she returned to the engineers. Her arrival caused a small flurry and she knew without being told that the pump was not quite ready.

'Another hour, Miss Wilton. We had a spot of bother. It'll be ready then.'

Sophie enjoyed her unaccustomed leisurely stroll around the shops, having time to talk with several friends, but was pleased when she was heading once again to Tiromaunga, the pump settled safely on the rear seat.

It was almost dark when she drove into the tree-lined drive, and as she was followed in by two other cars she was busy settling the guests immediately. Her father had let one of the units, she noted, as she entered the details before going to the living-room.

'I gather you had to wait for the pump,' her father smiled. 'Your Mr Roberts didn't turn up. The gardeners did, though. I wish you'd told me about it.'

'Gardeners?'

'Yes. They arrived shortly after you'd gone. A woodland area by the new drive is a pretty idea and bulbs are the way to go, but I wish you'd started with something a little more ordinary. Those Earlicheer narcissi are a dollar each, and five hundred of them, plus two gardeners digging . . .'

'What are you talking about? I never ordered any daffodils.'

'They asked for you, and the account's got your name on it. I left it on your desk in the office.'

Sophie's eyes widened. Jon Roberts had said she was like a spring flower; in fact, hadn't he mentioned Earlicheer? But it couldn't be? Not five hundred bulbs! She ran back to the office and found the envelope. It was not an account.

Her name was printed in a distinctive hand. Inside the single piece of paper contained a brief message:

> Winter is the season before spring,
> Jonathon Roberts.

Surprise deepened into anger. He wasn't being flattering. If he had wanted flowers he would have arranged for some from somewhere. He had compared her to a dried flower. She supposed there was a shade of improvement in being compared to a dormant plant!

'Jonathon Roberts!' she exploded to her father who had followed her. 'I'll root the whole lot out and send them back!'

Without waiting to think, she slammed out of the house and ran across the lawn to the drive. In the evening light it was impossible to make out where one had been planted. Frustrated, Sophie stamped back to the house.

'What am I going to do?'

'I thought you said you threw Jonathon Roberts out. Maybe the man thought he owed you an apology. It's a very imaginative one.'

'He wouldn't apologise under torture.' Sophie spoke vehemently. 'If I ask the gardeners to come back here to remove them I can't imagine what the charges will be, and if I dig the bulbs up myself it could take me weeks to find them.'

'There are five hundred. You'd never locate all of them. They've been damped and planted. The shop won't take them back. You'd better accept graciously.'

'If you think I'm going to write a polite thank-you to that . . . man, then think again. I'd like to send him five hundred stinging nettle plants! The only trouble is, you can't go into a shop and order them!'

Blonde hair bouncing indignantly, Sophie slammed the potatoes on to the bench. The vegetables were done in record time, the knife whizzing in her hand as she imagined what she would like to do to a certain male. To send her notice that spring came after winter! He was telling her that her personal difficult winter bereft of feeling was over; that he would make her blossom and that it would be earlier rather than later!

'Well, you're no busy little bee as far as I'm concerned, Jon Roberts; you're more like a wasp!' she muttered as she stirred the food.

It was not until much later in the evening that a faint memory made her go to the library and look up one of her grandfather's old plant books. Memory had not tricked her. She closed the book with a satisfied snap. Round two had definitely been Jon Roberts', but there was still time for one blow before the bell.

The letter took a long time to write, despite its brevity.

Dear Mr Roberts

This evening I returned home to find five hundred Earlicheer narcissi planted under our trees. Their significance is not lost. How clever of you to recall the Greek legend of the youth named Narcissus, who fell so in love with his own reflection in a pool that he refused to leave the spot. Despite reason and urgings from friends he ignored wisdom and remained. Eventually he grew roots and became the flower. As I have difficulty in seeing you as a small, frilly cream blossom I've realised the bulbs are not only an apology but also a message that you, unlike Narcissus, have listened to reason and are no longer interested in the site.

She signed her name with a graceful flourish and popped the page into the Tiromaunga envelope. A smile curved its way on her face and ended, dancing, in her eyes.

Although it was late, she decided to take the letter and the rest of the day's mail down to the post office. A quick run there and back would only take a few moments and the letter to Jon Roberts would be on its way!

The night air was freezing and her breath formed

little jets of steam as she ran down the drive and along the road. At the post office, her fingers slightly numbed, she had to stop to unzip her jacket to pull out the mail from her inside pocket. She posted the letters and gave the one to Jon Roberts, care of his Auckland hotel, a special thrust into the box.

'Sophie! This is a surprise.' David Alfield's pleasant voice startled her.

'I didn't know you were at home, David. How's life in the big city?'

'Come and have a drink and I'll tell you all about it, or about some of it,' he amended with a cheeky smile.

'I can't stay long.'

'I know. The lodge! No one's likely to turn up at this hour.'

The thought of Jon Roberts flashed into her mind and she shivered. David saw her action and he moved to her and put an arm around her shoulder.

'All right, just for a few minutes.'

They walked along the street to the hotel, chatting easily. Inside, several friends greeted them, and Sophie was turning towards a table when she froze. Sitting beside Harry was Jonathon Roberts!

CHAPTER THREE

BLUE eyes stared into Sophie's and an eyebrow rose, then Jon Roberts' glance shifted to the man at her side.

'Sophie! David! Come and join us.' Harry's brown eyes had lit with affection. He pulled out two chairs. 'You must meet Jon Roberts, just down from Auckland.'

Jon Roberts stood up, saying smoothly, 'I've met Sophie before,' and turned to extend his hand to David. As Harry completed the introduction Sophie was conscious of the men waiting for her to be seated. The ripple of blue mountain lake in Jon Roberts' eyes told her he knew very well she did not want to join him.

'Sophie and I were just discussing your excellent designs at Tiromaunga a few days ago, David. I told her I wanted to meet you.'

With David's pleasure obvious, Jon Roberts had forced her hand. She shot him an indignant glare and subsided on to the chair. Harry had left to get the drinks and David went to assist him.

'What are you doing here?' Sophie exploded.

'My dear young woman, you may be able to toss me out of your units, but you can't throw me out of the district, much as you may wish to!' His face

teased into a smile, crinkling the eyes that were so
blue. 'Have you abandoned your task for another
five minutes?'

'That's no business of yours.'

'Not yet, but I'm working towards it,' he said
smoothly. 'You really are quite enchanting to look
at. Your eyes have lightning sparks that flash like an
electric storm on a dark night. See, you just did it
again. Quite diverting!'

Sophie struggled to keep her temper in check. She
wasn't going to make a scene that would set the
whole neighbourhood talking, but she guessed Jon
Roberts wouldn't be above such a method if he felt it
would force her to leave the field. If he could control
himself, then she had to be the serene chatelaine of
Tiromaunga so she could keep up with him. She
wished Harry hadn't pushed her chair quite so
close to Jon's. At the small table there wasn't a great
deal of room, and she was too aware of her enemy's
strength beside her. As he leaned back, apparently
relaxed, she guessed she was the only person in the
room who would have known he was fully alert.

'My personal appearance is of no interest to you,
Mr Roberts,' she began crushingly, 'but I did just
post you a letter, acknowledging your decision and
apology.'

'I apologised?'

'The five hundred bulbs. Quite frankly, I was
surprised you had enough character to admit to your
appalling behaviour. I underestimated you.'

'Be careful, Sophie . . . you and I are like a pair of
warriors matched against each other. You can't win,

and I have no wish to hurt you severely.'

'You think I should just hand over now? Meekly surrender! There's no way you can touch my lodge, or me, either.' She saw the gleam in his eyes and hastily amended her words. 'At least, not without forcing yourself on me, and even you wouldn't risk that.'

'Wouldn't I?' He leaned forward and Sophie shot her chair back, almost upsetting Harry returning with the drinks.

'Let me take those, Harry.' Jon moved easily to take the glasses and at the same time Sophie saw him signal the barman. She wasn't surprised when another round appeared. She finished her first drink and deliberately made no move to touch the second. She wasn't having a thing provided by Jon Roberts, not even a drink in a bar.

For an instant the blue eyes flashed a challenge at her and she knew that, despite his interest in the conversation, Jon Roberts was watching her every movement.

'David, you stay here and talk.' She stood up when a natural pause in the conversation occurred. 'If you will excuse me.'

'Don't be absurd.' Jon Roberts had stood, too. 'You can't go home alone.'

'Why not? I'm not frightened by charging bulls,' she retorted.

'Sophie, you haven't touched your drink,' Harry said. 'Never mind, I'll polish it off for you.'

Sophie looked at Harry quickly. It was out of character for him; just how long had he been drink-

ing with Jon Roberts? More importantly, why was
Jon bothering with Harry? There had to be a reason.
She smiled when she realised Harry's land would be
second-best after their own block. Jon Roberts was
wasting his time. Nothing would induce Harry to
sell a few acres. His farm was even smaller than their
own! All the same, she wanted to separate Harry
from Jon Roberts.

'Harry, why don't you see me home? It's on your
way.'

Jon Roberts smiled at her as though acknowledging her effort. 'We'll all escort you. I feel like a walk
in the moonlight.' He looked at David and Harry.
'Coming?' Immediately they stood like eager
puppies.

Sophie silently muttered imprecations at the
manoeuvre. Jon was quick-witted, and not above
using his charm and position to manipulate.

'You know who Jon Roberts is, Sophie?' David
asked her quietly as Harry pointed out a local
landmark to Jon. 'Merely one of the top hoteliers in
the country! I couldn't believe my luck, running into
him. What do you think he's doing here? Wouldn't
it be fantastic if he wanted to set up one of his
millionaire resorts here? That's one contract I'd like
to do.'

'I think you'd be a front runner if he did. He
really admired the work you'd done at
Tiromaunga,' Sophie admitted. David's expression
told her of his hopes.

Harry and Jon rejoined them and they walked
briskly back to Tiromaunga, the night air chill, the

SPELL OF THE MOUNTAINS

men talking like old friends easily and naturally. Sophie knew a moment's dilemma as they approached the homestead. In other circumstances she would ask them in for a nightcap, but with Jon Roberts there she certainly wasn't!

'Now that's my idea of a house,' she heard Jon comment to David. 'Magnificent old place, just fits into the setting.'

'Sophie will show you over it. Though Theo is the real expert on Tiromaunga, isn't he?'

Sophie's search for an answer was interrupted by a dog's bark and the subsequent opening of the side door. Her father stood looking towards them. Reluctantly she introduced Jon Roberts and her father acknowledged him with a smile.

'Welcome. My daughter told me of your encounter! You'll all come in and have some supper, won't you?'

Sophie glared at Jon Roberts. His mouth twitched faintly in response. 'No, thank you, Mr Wilton. We just wanted to see Sophie home safely. I would like to call on you another day.' He shook hands, and David and Harry left with him.

'Seems a pleasant enough fellow,' her father commented as he shut the door.

'The rats probably said the same of the Pied Piper.'

'Don't worry, Sophie. He can't touch us.'

Sophie did not reply. She had told Jon she wouldn't touch him, yet he had held her and the memory still burnt. Jon Roberts would do exactly as he wanted!

The thought of the dark-haired, blue-eyed man accompanied her the following days. Each time she answered the lodge bell she found herself expecting him, and it was not until a week had passed that she began to relax. About the same time she began to miss Harry and their occasional outings. A good play was on in Christchurch at the Court Theatre, and it was one she particularly wished to see. In the past she knew Harry would have seen the advertisements and suggested a trip. Since discovering he loved her she had been careful not to ring him and, as luck would have it, she hadn't even run into him on one of her shopping expeditions. She could, of course, meet David or one of her old friends in Christchurch, but the prospect of driving back home alone late at night did not appeal. The alternative was to spend the night in town, but that would mean having to organise assistance for the guests in the morning . . . and with her luck it would be the time Jon Roberts would choose to talk to her father. Having seen Jon's expert manipulation at work, she wanted to make sure her father remained positive about not selling!

As a second and a third week passed she decided that Jon Roberts must have completely changed his mind. Oddly enough, the thought irritated; it was almost as if she wanted to see him again. She even went and inspected the area where the bulbs had been planted, but not even one green shoot showed under the blanket of leaves. The weather continued pleasant and each day showed the mountains, their tops covered with snow but not enough to enable the ski field to open.

Studying her early bookings, which were dependent on the open ski field, Sophie began to check the forecasts daily. Her father was as chirpy as a sparrow about the unaccustomed rate of grass growth and the consequent saving on winter feed. As the first and then the second cancellations started and then were followed by more, she became concerned. At the end of the month she showed her father the disastrous figures.

'It's never been as low, Dad. This time last year and the year before we've been searching for space for one more bed.'

'We'll make out, don't fret. The snow will come.'

Sophie could only hope. She had the occasional stray guest and a few regular clients, but there were too many days when the units were empty. In the beginning she kept busy springcleaning at Tiromaunga, giving the cupboards a thorough clean, checking stores and supplies, washing walls and curtains, and polishing panelling.

Even the gardens were looking tidy for the winter; the many plants had been clipped to root level, the trees had been trimmed in the driveway and the orchard had received a thorough pruning. The main vegetable garden had been dug over, the compost trenched and the edges straightened. For the first time since the units had been built, she had to look for work. As the beautiful sunlit days followed one another she felt prickles of concern when she studied her books.

'Last year we'd had skiers for six weeks by now,'

she commented to her father as she polished the hall brass.

'It opened three weeks early then. It's only three weeks late this year. You've been on a farm long enough to know you can't guarantee the weather. When it comes it'll probably make up for it by being a dumper.'

'Well, I hope it hurries up. The bank balance is looking worse with every day. I'm really getting concerned, Dad. If it goes on much longer I won't have enough in the account to make the quarterly repayments.'

'What do you intend to do about it?'

'Ask for an overdraft at the bank, I suppose. Our manager knows my record and the reason for the downturn. I'll be able to repay it fairly quickly once the season gets under way.'

'A bit disappointing for you. I'll have a look at the farm accounts closer to the time. I should have the cheque for the cattle soon. By the way, have you seen Harry since his holiday?'

'No. He told me he was going up north, but he was in a hurry at the time and he didn't finish telling me where and when.'

Her fingers slowed as she rubbed the large brass bowl, for once not amused by the funny lines her reflection had formed. Since she had known of Harry's love their meetings had been brief and constrained. She could only blame herself for not recognising the problem earlier. In time, Harry would come to terms with the situation, but she knew that her very awareness of his feelings made it harder for him. She realised her father was speaking.

'. . .decided to try fishing at Taupo. Not the lake, the river Kuratau. Jon Roberts jacked it up for him, I believe.'

'Jon Roberts?' Sophie was all attention. 'Was he here?'

'I'm not sure. He must have called on Harry.'

'There's something fishy going on,' she muttered. 'And Harry might be the bait being swallowed.'

'Harry's able to take care of himself. Although I understand that at the place where he was staying the idea is that you just enjoy yourself and the work's done for you. You catch the fish, but someone else prepares it for you. Harry was telling me the chef is supposed to be world class.'

'He was staying in the Millionaire Lodge?' Sophie swung round in surprise and her cloth caught the edge of the brass cleaner, sending it to crash on the floor. By the time she cleaned it up, her father had left to go round the few sheep he kept over the winter.

She made a cup of coffee and took it into her office. Everything was neat and tidy. The mail, with its refunds from cancellations, had been posted earlier. Not even Jon Roberts could do anything about the vacancies, she told herself. Or could he? Would he just sit back and accept the situation? Wouldn't he be trying to attract others? Hadn't he succeeded in prising Harry away from his home with the lure of fish and gourmet food? Could she manage something similar?

Didn't she have the Rakaia River right on her

doorstep? Wasn't it acknowledged as one of New Zealand's great salmon rivers? Would she be able to make a special offer; free accommodation for the weekend to the person who caught the biggest fish? Or the most salmon? She wrote the idea down and tried to think it through. Money for advertising could be a problem, but she should recoup her costs and it could be set off against the tax. 'Cost of advertising' she wrote beside the idea. 'Radio, newspaper, magazine'. A sudden thought made her laugh. The salmon season had ended earlier. Hadn't her father smoked the fish he had caught on the last day of the season? Still, she reflected, the idea was sound. Perhaps she could use it the following summer or autumn. And there could be other sports. Hadn't the golf tournament filled her lodge? The local club might be interested if she offered prizes for the best and worst score. She remembered the new walkway on Mount Somers. Would people be attracted to a weekend exploring some of the old mine areas and studying the geology of the area? Hadn't her father some of the semi-precious stones which had led an ill-informed miner to believe he had found diamonds? There could even be a treasure-hunt over a weekend, with different clues . . . Rapidly she covered the page with ideas.

Her coffee had gone cold when she next looked at the almost full mug. She felt exhilarated by the positive possibilities. Planning and co-ordinating everything would be much harder than merely thinking of the idea, but it was a start. The house and garden could spare her. House and garden?

Didn't they have carloads of people stopping just to drive slowly past the autumn glory of the trees? Could she have autumn tours, show off the gardens, giving a conducted tour to overnight guests? Perhaps she could include other local gardens. The Alfields' garden was Mr Alfield's joy, and he was the president of the local Horticultural Society; he was bound to know if people would be interested in such a day or two. She could organise such an occasion with demonstrations of rose-pruning or organic gardening methods or making pot-pourri. Wasn't Christchurch the garden city? A country weekend? Herbs . . .

The telephone buzzed beside her and she answered it quickly, hoping it would not be news of yet another cancellation.

'Good afternoon. This is Mr Roberts' secretary speaking. He has asked me to arrange an appointment with Mr Theo Wilton for tomorrow morning. After ten preferably, to fit in with flight times?'

Sophie's fingers tightened on the receiver. For so long she had been expecting Jon Roberts to arrive on the doorstep. She should have realised that he would use a formal approach. For a few seconds she was tempted to say her father would not be available, but she reasoned that it would only reveal her own fear. She had nothing to worry about. Her father was not interested in selling. If, in fact, Jon Roberts wanted to talk about the possibility; he could have purchased elsewhere, and perhaps was seeking her father's assistance with the area council.

'Would ten-thirty suit?' Her voice sounded tight.

'Ten-thirty? Thank you very much. Mr Roberts

will be at Tiromaunga at ten-thirty tomorrow.'

As she replaced the receiver, Sophie once more repeated to herself the fact that the units were safe. Her father needed more land, not less. As for Jon's ridiculous threat that he would take her, too; she wasn't going to waste any more time thinking about it.

'Perhaps Jon Roberts has heard what a great ski season we're having and decided against setting up in Methven,' her father teased when she told him of the telephone call. 'Don't worry, Sophie, I'm not going to sell him one inch, let alone several acres.'

Sophie had never known time to drag so slowly. It was a relief when two regulars arrived, and she was kept busy for a short time! After dinner she found it impossible to watch television, and after making two attempts to read she gave up and poked moodily at the flickering fire in the lounge.

'You're as jumpy as a kitten up a tree. Jon Roberts is only a man.'

'So was Machiavelli.'

Her father's snort of laughter helped. The old house creaked and both looked at one another.

'Change of wind. Maybe you'll have your snow soon.'

'It was warm today,' Sophie recalled.

'Hope I didn't make a mistake putting those sheep in the end paddock. If we get bad weather in the morning I'll have to shift them up, nearer home. I don't want to have to go miles to feed out, in the event of a smattering of snow falling here.'

'We haven't had any snow down here for the past seven years.'

'And long may that continue. Snow's all right on
mountains and Christmas cards.'

'I'm not even sure about the Christmas cards. From
the northern hemisphere it seems right, because
they're having winter.' She wondered how Jonathon
Roberts spent Christmas. Did he have a family? There
had been no mention of them in the article. It was hard
to picture him with a mother and father and brothers
and sisters—though she could visualise him as a small
boy with thoughtful blue eyes and a mop of unruly
hair. He would have been so cuddly and lovable.
Somewhere along the line he had changed. He had
hardened as he grew up, become able to handle
situations and manipulate people. But what was she
doing thinking about him? Didn't she detest him?
Why did her thoughts continually return to him?

The crying of the wind in the trees disturbed her
several times in the night. When she woke she pulled
back the curtains beside her bed and peered out
hopefully. The sun was still sleeping with his blankets
of cloud and mist. Joy lifted her heart. The mountains
were white. The snow had been given, not in miserly
patches, but in munificent white heaps. Even the lower
bush was covered.

When she had showered and dressed she studied the
scene more carefully. It looked magnificent, the great,
white peaks soaring into the clouds, steep-sided black
rocks contrasting with the snow. Her eyes sped to the
place where usually the access road could be clearly
seen, and disappointment scalded her. The road
winding through the mountains was invisible. There

would be no skiing until the road was clear. Even as she stood there watching, the mists and clouds rolled down the mountains to the plains, covering the sight like a theatre's great curtain.

Her father was already up when she went to the kitchen.

'Morning, Sophie.' He poured the porridge. 'I think we might be in for trouble later in the day.'

'I know we are,' Sophie answered, thinking of the ten-thirty appointment.

'I'll need you to give me a hand. I'm going to shift the sheep up to the woolshed.'

Sophie's smile at the misinterpretation died.

'Under cover? But why?'

'I hope I'm wrong. But the sky reminds me of the time of the big blizzard when I was fourteen. We only saved the stock we managed to get under shelter. Several farmers were wiped out. Phone the Alfields and suggest they do the same. Tell them to pass the word on. Give Harry a ring too.' Her father looked again at the sky and shook his head. 'You'd better park the big tractor in the house garage too. We might need it if the snow is feet thick. I'm off!'

'I'll open up the woolshed for you,' Sophie promised.

He finished his porridge and Sophie decided to let hers cool a little while she telephoned. Mrs Alfield answered promptly, readily understanding. Neither wasted words. She tried Harry's number but it rang on uninterrupted. She replaced the receiver, hoping that he was already out shifting his stock. As she ate her porridge she realised she would have to inform the clients at the lodge. If they left immediately they could be back in Christchurch before the storm cut off access. She flung on her thick coat and hat and ran to check. The unit was empty; the occupants had realised the situation. She ran for the tractor and parked it in the house garage, then climbed into the truck.

The occasional snowflake spangled the cab as she drove it to the woolshed. Working rapidly she opened the gates and pens to let the sheep into the shed.

Her father was in sight, but she had time to try Harry. She drove back to the homestead, conscious that the sky was closing in. She looked towards Harry's farm and noted the sheep moving to the shelter of the line of pines. Couldn't Harry see that even the animals knew the weather was going sour? She tried his telephone again and was almost shocked when he answered.

'Don't panic, Sophie. We've had snow before. It's like confetti at a wedding, a sprinkle or two. It won't hurt the sheep.'

'Dad thinks it will.' Rapidly she relayed her father's words. 'I have to go, I can hear the dogs and Dad's farm bike.'

Snow was beginning to mark the outlines of the ground. For a moment she wondered if Harry could be right, so she glanced again at the sky. Grey-white clouds hung low, heavy and swollen. For the first time she knew a trace of fear; she had never seen the sky look so oppressive. She reached the woolshed just as the sheep were moving towards the outer race. The barks of the dogs seemed oddly loud. As the sheep moved in she began penning up, making sure the numbers to each pen allowed sufficient room, and swinging the gates into position. For once the sheep seemed just as keen to be shedded up.

'That's it.'

'Thanks, Sophie. Did you get hold of the Alfields?'

'Yes, they were about to ring us to see if you'd ever seen the conditions. They should have most of their stock heading in. David's home, so he can muster too.' She paused. 'I've only just managed to get hold of Harry. He laughed at the idea.'

Her father looked anxious. 'Stupid young . . .' He looked again at the sky. 'Those clouds look pregnant. We've been lucky they haven't dropped their bundles so far.' He looked sombrely towards the boundary. 'I can't stand by and let stock die. Ring him up, tell him to get off his backside if he doesn't want to spend the next week snowraking. I'll muster his canal paddock; there are no trees there to shelter his ewes, so that's the most urgent.'

He revved the farm motorbike and called his best dog to jump into position on the pillion. There was no time to appreciate the skill and balance necessary. Sophie turned to the truck and drove it back to the house.

The sight of the vehicle parked by the office door pulled her up with a jolt. Hastily she glanced at her watch. It was ten-forty. Jonathon Roberts opened the car door as she approached.

'I forgot you were coming.' She saw the blue eyes widen a little in patent disbelief. 'I'm sorry, I think you'd better come some other time. Dad's busy. I'd advise you to leave now.'

'I've just flown down from Auckland for this appointment and I'm prepared to wait until your father sees me.' His blue eyes showed contempt. 'I thought you would have told your father about the appointment.'

'I did. I haven't time to argue. Can't you see that sky?' Without waiting to see if he followed or not, she ran to the rear door, stopping only to kick off her gumboots on the porch. Seconds later she was dialling Harry's number. There was no reply, but she let it ring.

She heard the rear door close and knew Jon Roberts had followed her inside. A wry smile spread over her face. For so long she had worried about meeting him, she had lain awake half the night dreading the appointment, yet when the time came she had forgotten!

'If someone was there they would have had time to answer by now.' Jon Roberts took the phone from her hand. The intimate contact jolted her.

'Is something wrong? Can I help?'

Sophie looked at him. In his immaculate hand-tailored suit he looked as if he had stepped from the fashion page of a glossy magazine.

'In that?' she scorned. His expression told her she had to give him an explanation and fast. 'We've shedded up. Put the sheep in the woolshed,' she said. 'Dad thinks we're in for the hundred-year snowstorm. He's gone to help next door. Harry will lose a lot of his stock if he doesn't get them under cover, if Dad's right. You'd better go to the hotel.

I'll get Dad to ring you when he gets back. I'm off to help.'

'Stop! Give me three minutes and some old clothes of your father's.'

Sophie looked at him in surprise.

'Hurry up, you're wasting time.'

Sophie thought quickly. If Jon Roberts wanted to help Harry, he could. The extra man would be useful.

'Come on, then.' She led the way to her father's bedroom and rapidly sorted out some farm clothes from his dressing-room. Jon Roberts had stripped down to his underpants and socks by the time she handed over the clothes.

'Give me your keys. I'll put your car under cover temporarily. I don't want it stuck here.'

'Right-hand trouser pocket. Wouldn't it be faster to use it to get across to Harry's?'

'We'll take the truck and go across the paddocks.' Going through the still warm pocket, she found the keys immediately. She left the room with alacrity, glad of the excuse to hurry. Jon Roberts in a suit was impressive, but stripped he was beautiful. He looked like a classic Greek statue come to life: proud head, developed chest, lean hips, limbs muscled into power. She smiled a little, understanding how Narcissus had fallen in love with his own reflection!

The car opened to her touch and she slipped into the driver's seat. It took a few seconds to readjust the seat. Jon Roberts' legs were several inches longer than her own. Even in her hurry she drank in the soft leather upholstery, the craftsman-like finish, the easily read rev. counter. The motor surged as she gave it power and she eased back quickly, changing gear smoothly as the car rolled gently forward. The wheel responded to her guide effortlessly and she felt a tinge of envy well up in her as she enjoyed driving it into the old stables. She switched off the motor and locked the car automatically, then shut the giant doors. Jon hadn't taken long to change. Running, she gestured him to the truck. Two of the dogs barked hopefully, and she whistled them aboard as she climbed into the passenger seat.

'Which way?'

'Left, then diagonally across to the boundary gate.' It seemed strange to be seated beside Jon Roberts, bouncing across the almost white paddocks, the windscreen wipers flicking away the occasional flake. She risked a side glance at him, just as he turned his head and their eyes met.

'Not exactly Gentleman Jim!' he admitted.

'Dad's six feet tall, so you must be a couple of inches more, judging by the trousers and sleeves. Don't worry, the sheep won't mind.' A particularly hard bump made her gasp in protest.

'Sorry, must have been a log or something. Bit difficult to see under the snow.'

'Look, there's Harry!'

With relief Sophie realised the mob was more than half-way to the safety of the woolshed. The sheep were moving fast, dogs and men urging them forward, the motors, voices and the dogs' barks muffled by the snow.

'You drive. I'll get out and help.'

Sophie slid over and took control of the truck without protest. She didn't envy the men hustling the sheep forward in the rapidly chilling conditions. She watched for a moment, then realised that the leading sheep were uncertain of their route, their senses disturbed by the unfamiliar conditions. Making a wide cast with the truck, she put the truck at the head of the mob and began making a path across the white paddock directly to the stock yards. She drove slowly and was relieved to see the sheep following readily when she checked her rear-vision mirror.

At the yards she stopped and climbed down from the cab. The cold hit her, lung-tingling gasps of cold air, sapping her body-heat and numbing her fingers as she tried to lug open the heavy old stock gates. Her gumboots skidded against the slushy mud of the outer yard as she pushed all her strength against the weatherworn gates. When they gave, she hurled herself at the next one, mentally promising Harry Southton a lecture on the benefits of yard gates that worked, even if you weren't six feet tall and with a Clydesdale's muscles.

Snowflakes were falling on her face and running wetly down the back of her collar as she reached the woolshed. By the time she had opened the doors of the pens she could see that the sheep had almost reached the yards. Her father's signal summoned her back to the truck.

'Sophie. Take Jon out while you can. He's booked into the pub. I'll stay and help Harry get the mob in, and then I'll ride straight home.'

Sophie watched as her father and Harry waved their thanks to Jon, and a moment later he climbed frozenly aboard the truck. Remembering her own short time in the cold, she began to feel a slight sympathy.

'I'll boost the heater.' She switched it on high and swung the truck back towards Tiromaunga. Jon peeled off the wet hat, his dark hair pressed monk-like against his scalp, the skin on his face thawing, turning shades of blue, purple and orange. She had driven through the boundary gateway when the snow fall began suddenly to frighten her. The windscreen wipers were no longer able to brush away the flakes.

A bank of snow began building up underneath the screen. Sophie had to strain to pick up marks to give her definition, the window was almost useless.

'Use the fence lines,' Jon's voice cut in. 'It may be slightly longer, but at least you'll be able to follow them back.'

'Don't worry, I've no intention of getting myself stranded here with you. I know exactly where I am,' she answered as they passed the second gateway. The shelterbelt began beside it, to Sophie's relief. She hadn't wanted to admit that she had been alarmed by the white-out. The protection of the old pines filtered the worst of the snow, enabling the wipers to restore vision while Sophie kept the truck as close to the belt as she could.

'These go all the way to the homestead,' she told Jon. 'You're quite safe.'

Only as they drove into Tiromaunga's yard did she realise it would be impossible for Jon to leave.

'You'll have to come in until it clears,' she admitted grudgingly. 'It shouldn't be long.'

'Your gracious invitation is accepted.' His blue eyes were apparently innocent of guile, but Sophie felt uneasy and threatened by his presence.

CHAPTER FOUR

SOPHIE drove the truck into the garage and climbed down from the cab. 'Come on, we can go along the veranda to the kitchen.' She had reached the sanctuary of the kitchen when she heard a mournful bellow. She stopped in the act of removing her jacket.

'We've forgotten the bull. I'll have to get some hay . . .'

'Now I've heard everything! The bull will be fine. There's an old shed in his paddock, under the trees.'

She looked at him, recalling that he was right. He had done his homework thoroughly. The reminder did not endear him, but she had to admit he had worked hard in difficult conditions. As a result he was saturated.

'Use Dad's shower. I'll get you some towels and some more clothes. You're soaked through.'

She had just handed him the gear when the telephone went. Sophie sped to it and was relieved to hear her father's voice.

'Sophie? You made it! Thank God! I've never seen anything like the snow we had five minutes after you left.'

'It was tricky; I followed the trees.'

'Good thinking. I wasn't even sure if you would

have got that far. I was worried about you. Jon will have to sit it out too, I'm afraid. I'll come home as soon as it's safe, but in the meantime I'll stay with Harry.'

'Fine, Dad. I'm just off to have a shower. I'll ring you later.'

She was shivering despite the warmth of the house, and it was a relief in the shower to let the hot water run and play on her skin. She dressed in a thick jersey and shirt as well as her jeans, and padded out to the kitchen.

Jon Roberts appeared, fresh and clean and ruddy-faced, as she was preparing a drink.

'Your father and Harry OK?'

'Fine. We have to thank you for your assistance.' Blue eyes studied her and she stood as tall as she could.

'I've a vested interest.' His mouth twitched slightly. 'I'd appreciate a hot drink and I'd like to use the phone. It appears I may be here for a while.'

Sophie viewed him with dismay, then turned hopefully to look at the driveway. She glanced out of the hall window, then looked again. In the short time they had been inside, the outside world had changed.

'Oh, no!' Her cry described her feelings.

'Exactly!' Jon Roberts sounded equally grim.

The air was full of floating snowflakes, as if a giant hand was throwing thousands of white chrysanthemum petals over the house. With a shock Sophie realised that she could not even see the shrubs in the border garden a mere four feet from the window.

Jon Roberts wouldn't be able to leave Tiromaunga, possibly for a day or more. Worse, she would be alone with the man.

He was standing by the telephone, and she realised he was waiting for her to go. She shut the hall door behind her with slightly more force than was necessary. Surely Jon Roberts had not thought she would be the least bit interested in his conversations?

She began making some hot chocolate, and it was ready when Jon entered the kitchen.

'Thank you.' He took the mug and stood with his back to the kitchen burner which was throwing out a good heat. Sophie found she was aware of the watchful gaze.

'Help yourself to some more chocolate.' She gestured to the pot. 'I'll just organise some food for lunch. You'll be hungry.'

'At the moment I feel I could eat anything as long as it's warm,' he admitted. 'I've never been so cold.'

She finished fine-chopping the vegetables, deftly adding them to the pan and stir-frying them. She warmed two plates and set the kitchen table.

'We usually eat in the dining-room, but it's warmer in here.'

'Definitely here. After lunch I'd like to telephone your father. I've an offer for him.'

'He's not interested in selling.' Sophie was completely confident.

'People can change their minds.'

Reminding herself that her father had no need to sell, she turned back to the stove and began to dish up. 'It's ready. You can sit there.' She pointed to her father's chair and he left his stand by the burner to take a chair.

Sophie switched on the radio in an endeavour to cover the strange silence that seemed to blanket them. Jon Roberts was extremely courteous, holding her chair, passing her the condiments, making the occasional comment, but Sophie was too aware of her own feelings to be comfortable.

'The food was excellent.' Jon picked up her plate and his own and put them on the bench. His mouth twisted into a semblance of a smile. 'Relax, Sophie. I'd rather cuddle a hedgehog than touch you.'

It was not a compliment, but Sophie found the remark reassuring.

'Can I ring your father from here?' He pointed to the kitchen telephone.

'If you like.' She told him the number and then moved to tidy away the remains of the meal. She heard Jon talk easily to Harry, then asked to speak to her father. As she wiped down the bench she couldn't help hearing her father's voice express thanks for seeing her safely back to Tiromaunga. She would have been quite competent by herself, she thought, aggrieved.

'I'll have to stay here. What would you like done about feeding the stock? Yes, I'm sure we can manage. It will depend on the storm. At the moment the snow is still coming; we can't see the edge of the veranda from where I'm standing.'

Jon was listening to her father, and Sophie began to move towards the hall door.

'Wait, Sophie. I want you to hear this.' He spoke again. 'I came to see you about the lodge. I'd like to outline my plan. You do know I'm ready to buy it? Sophie told me you wouldn't consider selling as you need more land, is that correct? It is? Now, I've been discussing the situation with Harry. I gather his farm is too small to offer him a challenge and to be economic much longer. He has some excellent ideas and it would be a waste if he can't put them to use. While he was up north I showed him a farm with considerable potential in the Manawatu. He's very keen to buy it, but the value of his place here wouldn't fetch enough on the open market. I've told him that I'd be prepared to set him up in return for his farm. What I'm offering you is a swap. I want the six units and thirty acres, but in return I'll give you Harry's farm and stock, minus the cottage, and the five acres it stands on.'

Sophie spun round, open-mouthed. Jon listened, then spoke again. 'Yes, that's it. I'm sure you realise the value of the units. I have independent reports here which I hoped to show you, but the storm has made it impossible. But I guess you know the value of Harry's land and stock better than any outsider.'

Sophie felt her world begin to shake. Jon Roberts was so plausible, she thought. He had the fattest carrot to dangle in front of her father. No, not one carrot, a whole farmload of them. More land! And not just any land. Harry's place, the farm which was adjoining theirs. How could she plead against that?

There had to be a way. Given time, she would come up with the answer.

'No, unfortunately that's the one thing I can't give you. Normally, of course, you'd have time to consider every angle, but the farmer in Manawatu has given me an option until six o'clock tonight for Harry, and if that falls through the whole deal is off. Time is of the essence. I'm worried about the storm cutting the communication links. I'd like to send off a telex to the farmer as soon as possible.'

Sophie could not believe what was happening. Jon Roberts was forcing her father to make an immediate decision!

'The thirty acres? Yes, the land on which the units are set and the front ten acres, including a share of the driveway as far as and including the turn-off to the units. The rest takes it to the end of the bull paddock. It's not quite thirty acres, twenty-nine point seven.'

Sophie saw the blue eyes gleam and knew she had lost unless she acted swiftly. She made a movement and Jon spoke again.

'Sophie's here. I thought it best if she heard my offer. I'll pass her the phone now.'

'Dad?' Her voice came out in a rush. 'Think about it. Take time.'

'Sophie, I don't need to think. It's what I've dreamt about. The whole deal is wonderful. I get the land and stock, and all it costs me is the thirty acres and the units. It's an incredible offer.'

'The units!'

'They'll still be there. He'll probably want you to go on running them,' he laughed. 'Proper hours and real wages, too! Tell him I accept his offer. No, better still, let me talk to him and thank him myself.'

Sophie held out the receiver to Jon Roberts, conscious of his silent appraisal of her defeat. It was hard to speak the word. 'Congratulations!'

'Thank you, Sophie.' He took the phone. 'Good! Glad you're pleased. Yes, it has to be in writing. Send a telex to my Auckland office and they'll let the Manawatu farmer know. As soon as that's received, word will be sent to Harry informing him the Manawatu place is his officially.'

Sophie slipped out of the kitchen and Jon Roberts made no move to detain her. He had won! The units had been sold. The impossible had become reality in a matter of a few seconds. Jon Roberts hadn't needed to sell the idea. Her father had jumped at the exchange. He hadn't taken two minutes to think it all through, let alone check the value of the units on the open market.

Jon Roberts hadn't given him time. He had pressured her father with the knowledge that Harry was interested in one farm and this was the one opportunity. He had even used the storm as a lever . . .

She walked down the hall and into the office at the end of the wing. It was always one of the favourite rooms in the old house, with its glass on three sides and its turret corner. When she had needed an office she had turned her old playroom into a more formal room, but it retained its air of solid warmth and happiness. From the turret she usually had a view towards the tree-lined garden and drive and one end of the units.

The white curtain of snow hung down, blocking everything. At her desk her fingers flipped over the three letters she had written the previous night acknowledging deposits for later in the season. At the time, she had been pleased to receive tangible proof that the snow would come and that her accounts would improve. It no longer meant anything.

Also on the desk was the range of curtain samples, and the swatches of colour seemed appropriate. She had been like a child with a balloon, and Jon Roberts had come along and in one thrust had left her with scraps.

The telephone buzzed and she eyed it sadly. She knew exactly what it meant. The sale had gone through. She picked it up and answered mechanically.

'Person-to-person call for Jonathon Roberts. Is he available, please?'

'One moment, I'll put you through.' She guessed he would still be in the kitchen. She connected the call and replaced the phone when she heard his voice.

The light on the board told her when the call was finished, but the phone lit almost immediately, telling her he was dialling out. She moved away, guessing he was calling her father and Harry.

Why had Harry decided to sell? What had happened to change his mind? She had known Jon Roberts was up to something when they had met at the hotel, but she had been so certain Harry would not sell . . .

'Sophie?'

Jon Roberts walked into the room bearing a silver tray, glasses and a long green bottle. Sophie looked at him, then at the tray. It could only mean one thing. He had won!

'Your father suggested we should celebrate.'

'Celebrate?' She felt like throwing the lot at him. Jon put the tray on the desk.

'I've had acknowledgement through my Auckland office. Your father didn't waste time agreeing to my terms. Harry's pleased, too.'

'And you?' Sophie's feelings were raw.

'I knew I would win. My pleasure came when I knew Harry was interested in the farm my staff had found for him up north. That was the key.' He poured out the golden, bubbling fluid into two fine glasses and handed her one.

'I don't feel like celebrating your victory.'

'Please yourself! Though I can recommend the wine. It could be a degree or two colder for perfection, but that shouldn't worry you. Just let it stand by you for a while and it'll develop icicles.'

Sophie bit back her retort. She didn't want Jon Roberts to see her anguish.

He walked over to the window and stared out at the still falling snow before turning and studying her. Sophie felt his dissatisfaction and irritation.

'I don't like being stuck here with you, either.'

'I know, if you could, you'd throw me out! You're going to have to get used to seeing me around, my dear Sophie.'

'I am not your dear Sophie,' she exploded. 'I detest you. You don't care about me.'

'Why should I? You're an intelligent young woman with a fair share of charm and attraction. I'm not poor old Harry, content to be your lap dog, grateful for your occasional company and a meal!'

'That's unfair. I'm very fond of Harry. I never knew he loved me until . . .' She stopped, aware of Jon's interest.

'And you told him there was no chance. So that's how it happened.' Jon spoke almost to himself. 'My experts couldn't get any assistance from Harry, then I came through and found a whole new game on the board. Instead of wanting to stay, he wanted desperately to get away from you for a few days.'

'You manipulated him.'

'If you like. But Harry will be able to explore a lot of other possibilities. You told me yourself his farm was too small, and my reports bore that out.'

'I hadn't forgotten your spies.'

'Experts, doing a job they were paid to do. A feasibility study. You don't imagine I go pouring millions into a proposition that hasn't been tested? I'm not a fool.'

'That much I will concede,' Sophie admitted, her feelings bruised and battered. Automatically she finished her glass of wine and Jon refilled it. Sadly she realised that she had given the key to Jon. She had reinforced his reports about the farm and the need for land. She had even handed him Harry at his most vulnerable.

'Are you telling me that if Harry hadn't sold, you would have used somewhere else?'

Jon looked at her coolly before replying. 'Do

you really want the answer to that? If it helps, I did have another way of getting the units.'

Sophie looked at him in disbelief. 'How?'

'You.'

'Me?'

'The sacrifice would have been considerable, but I was considering it.' His lips curled into a twisted smile. 'Marriage, Sophie. You and me.'

'You're mad!'

'I thought we'd agreed I wasn't a fool.'

'But I can't stand you, and you don't even like me.'

'Given time, I could make you love me. It would have been a marriage made not in heaven, but at our lawyers. You'd have brought the deeds to the units as a wedding gift from your father.' His cynicism was clear in a small laugh.

'The idea's preposterous.'

'No. Just a little lateral thinking on my part.' His eyes roved over her and he smiled. 'Or should I say horizontal?'

'And you imagined I'd go along and say . . .'

'I do. I can be persuasive. Most women make passes at me.' He ran his hand through his neatly cut hair.

'I'll be able to resist the temptation!'

'Such certainty. Can I remind you of something? You'll be kissing me before midnight's struck. Just how far you'll go after that . . .'

'You arrogant chauvinist! I wouldn't kiss you if . . .'

She broke off suddenly, remembering something.

Hadn't she made some bet with Jon Roberts . . .
something about kissing a snake, if he was able to
buy the units before her birthday.

'You haven't much choice, have you? There are
no snakes in New Zealand.' His grin contained
triumph. 'Would you prefer to get it over and done
with, or would you rather take the opportunity to get
to know me a little further?'

'You're enjoying this . . .'

'Of course I am.'

'You wouldn't insist on . . .'

'You keeping your side of the wager? Yes. Yes, I
would.' He walked towards her and she moved
away, fearful, but determined not to let him see
it.

'I wouldn't go within an arm's reach of you.'

'My arms are longer than yours.'

'Don't you dare touch me.'

'I'll give you till a minute before midnight. I don't
think you could do a lot to stop me if I wanted to
make love to you. There would be no point in
screaming; no one would hear and the snow
prevents you leaving.'

'I've done self-defence.' Sophie crossed her
fingers behind her back.

'I'd hardly think your instructor would agree.
You did begin the course and attended two lectures,
then you met Pierre Cascelt and gave up on the self-
defence. Strikes me you'd have been better off in the
class.'

'I would have gone for a black belt if I'd known
I was going to be stuck here with you, a body-

builder's dream, with half a brain!'

When she saw the anger in his eyes, she wished she had held her temper in leash.

'Half a brain?' The ice in his voice struck terror into her. She had to keep him at bay with definite reasons.

'You're like a superb robot . . . a robot without a programme for compassion and love and trust. You use people and situations. I'm sorry. I guess something must have gone wrong somewhere, some time.'

'Spare me your melodramatic outpourings of sympathy.'

Sophie turned away, knowing he was back in control of himself. He might have mocked, but she was sure she had been correct.

'I don't let emotions interfere with business.' He finished the glass of wine and offered her more, but she still had a full glass.

'You don't trust me very far, do you?'

'I haven't seen any reason.'

'Good, you're learning.'

'To you this whole deal has just been another challenge. You could have built your motel on Harry's land and sold my father the acres you didn't need.'

'That wouldn't have been the best option.'

'Best option? Who for? You? The bank? For more money?'

'Yes. My set-up would have totally ruined your units' viability, and I couldn't have stepped in to buy you out. It was part of the wager, remember?'

He moved back to the window and glared again at the storm. 'But don't be misled. I set up the deal to get the best result and I achieved it. It's not my policy to accept second place.'

Sophie set her glass carefully on the tray. 'But you expect me to?'

'I have nothing to do with your place. You carved your own hollow.'

'Come on . . .'

'Your mistake was not having your name on the titles. You should have insisted on that from the beginning.'

'But it was my father's land and capital . . .'

'Exactly! You should have demanded a partnership, as your father was virtually a sleeping partner. According to my information, your father never did any work in the units. Alternatively, with your salary as manageress you should have started to buy your father out, or you could have taken a share instead of a larger wage.'

Sophie felt pain from his suggestion. She certainly wasn't going to tell Jon Roberts that her wages had been nominal.

'I suppose if you had been wearing my shoes you would have had a multi-million-dollar motel out there by now?'

'Yes.' He sounded so confident, so assured of his own invincibility, Sophie was incensed.

'How?' The single question burst from her.

It was a minute or two before Jon began to answer her. 'I've already told you, I would have asked for a share in the first units. I would have banked all the monies with the local bank. They have a lower mortgage repayment rate than the private loan your father arranged. Once the first year's record had been established I would have negotiated a new mortgage with them covering another set of four units. The deposit would have come from my salary and in part from my share of the capital gain of the first units.'

'After the first year?' Sophie heard herself ask.

'Yes. The capital growth factor is a very important one. Assets usually increase faster than the inflation rate. Simple economics. With the growth of the business you can afford to expand; more units mean more money, which in turn reaps more capital growth. You offset the interest against tax as well as the expenditure.'

'You make it sound simple. What about coming unstuck? Outrunning your liquidity?'

'I wouldn't have done that as I'd check the need first. The feasibility study, remember? In the case of Tiromaunga you could hardly go wrong. The ski season lasts for months, and while that's on you could sell every bed several times. Guaranteed occupancy is an innkeeper's dream.'

'There's still the rest of the year.'

'Granted. Again it's a matter of knowing the market and the potential and resources available. One of the fastest-growing sections is the recreational tourist area. I'd develop that side. People like to have fun, and the more fun and excitement, the better.'

'What's wrong with simply providing a calm,

quiet, clean place to stay?'

'That's essential. But most people want a selection of other options as well.'

'You've forgotten a small but salient fact. Dad wouldn't release any more land.'

'I hadn't forgotten, merely discounted it. To begin with, you could have built a further four units on the top of the present block. Or if you didn't want to do that, you could have built two units on the present turn-around area and set two above them. According to my plans you would have still room to turn a coach, and you would have only taken a further five feet of farm land. All that landscaping might look attractive, but to say that you've under-utilised the land available is putting it mildly. I don't blame your father for refusing.'

Sophie stared glumly out of the window, but the white glare stung and she turned back to face her tormentor. 'I'm sure you could have done better!'

'Yes, I'd employ an expert,' he said crushingly. 'You're a product of your own environment, Sophie. Your family has been here over a hundred years, but you're dealing with a different situation. Your clients arrive and go within a day or two. Most of them would be unaware of all your shrubs and trees.'

'You're wrong there.' Sophie faced him. 'Just about everyone who comes comments on the attractive gardens around the units.'

'In some spots extra garden can create a feeling of openness and space, but when you already have such a view and the bonus of the trees of Tiromaunga beside you, the fact remains that a lot of it is unproductive and unnecessary from a financial point of view.'

'I might have guessed! Money! With you, it always comes back to the dollar.'

'If you'd considered your position more carefully from that point of view, you wouldn't be in the mess you are!'

The statement, made coolly and implacably, fired Sophie's antagonism again. She knew that Jon Roberts was right, and she was fast beginning to loathe his certitude.

'So, Mr Expert, tell me what happens next?' she said crushingly.

'If you're referring to the units, the only thing to concern you is the settlement date. I arranged it to be the day before your twenty-fourth birthday.'

'You mean that's when the legal documents are handed over and the money and so forth?'

'Yes.' He looked at her and Sophie remembered to hurriedly change the subject.

'I thought you would want to see the books and so on.'

'My staff would normally do that. Usually they investigate that before a deal, but as this is going to be a very different property it isn't really so important.'

'So it's no good my offering to show you the files now?'

'On the contrary, that would be a profitable way of spending the time as far as I'm concerned.'

Sophie thought quickly. If Jon Roberts was

interested, the books would keep him entertained and she could retire with dignity. She went to the desk and pulled open her files.

'Here you are.' She was acutely aware of his presence beside her as he studied the first entries. 'Do you want me to stay? To clarify anything?'

'It looks logical. It's a long time since I did this sort of operation without a computer, but I believe I'll cope.'

'The earlier books are in the first cupboard. You're welcome to study those, too, if you wish. You can help yourself to any other papers you require.'

He nodded and sat down behind her desk as though he owned that, too. Sophie walked out. Jon Roberts sitting at her desk, going through her books, was suddenly too much. Tears stung her eyes. Once she had closed the door behind her she stopped the effort of maintaining her dignity and ran along the hall to her bedroom, the tears finally flowing unchecked.

Her bright, shiny, beautiful dream had been smashed. Jon Roberts had held the bait her father had been unable to resist. Her pillow was damp when she sat up again on her bed, hoping she hadn't heard her name being called. Instinctively she brushed the last tears from her eyes.

'Sophie! Telephone!' The voice was peremptory.

She sniffed hastily. 'Coming,' she acknowledged. She listened as the footsteps strode back down the passage to the office. She could take the call in the kitchen without Jon knowing her tears. She had her pride, even if she held little else.

She answered the telephone quietly and the click of the office switch told her Jon had closed his line. Again she was aware of her shoulders relaxing. What was it about the man that she tensed every time they met?

The sound of Mrs Alfield's voice asking if she was feeling all right made her pause. She was very tempted, but she knew her father would want to tell the Alfields himself face to face. While she was trying to think of the right words, the line went dead. Either Jon Roberts had cut her call or the snow had brought down the wires. She tapped the buttons, but the dialling tone was gone.

Somehow the loss of the last link seemed to make the isolation worse. Why couldn't the phone have been cut two hours earlier? Even the weather had assisted Jon Roberts!

Sophie opened the kitchen door. The veranda was sufficient protection for her to risk the white petals still falling incessantly. Even on the mountain in a short white-out, she had never seen such a snow fall. The cold shock of the weather slapping her face made her hurriedly retreat. She was satisfied on one point. There would be no attempt to feed the stock while the snow was falling in such quantities. Sooner or later it would stop and she could go and check their condition. A rueful smile crossed her face as she realised she would probably sink several times in attempting the distance. It was just as well the tractor was handy! Her father and Harry would be facing a similar problem, but at least the sheep were safe.

While she waited she would have to prepare a meal. She felt very much like throwing Jon a can opener and a tin of baked beans. The thought that he would probably ignore it and cook himself something else changed her mind. She would not let him have the satisfaction of knowing just how much she had been hurt. Instead she would play his game of cool self-possession, hiding her real feelings.

She studied the fresh ingredients, then checked her deep freeze. There was enough to last them for a dozen blizzards, she noted thankfully. Jon Roberts might have lanced her with the sale, but he would have difficulty picking holes in her skill with food. Her mother hadn't been a Women's Institute prize-winning cook for nothing!

An hour and a half later Sophie set the last fork in perfect position on the dining-table. She smiled as she viewed the long formal table with a place set at either end. For the first time she was glad about the fifteen children of her ancestors. At least the gap separating her from Jon Roberts was illustrated well!

She checked the sauce and the soup, then went to change. If she was going to act the lady of Tiromaunga she had to dress appropriately, especially as she knew Jon Roberts had no spare clothes with him! In her long cream woollen skirt and soft lacy cream mohair and lambswool jersey, and with her hair plaited back, she entered the office. Jon stopped in mid-calculation.

'The snow queen herself, I presume.' His eyes flicked over her. 'Look, but don't touch.'

'That's right, Mr Roberts. Dinner will be ready in ten minutes,' she announced, then, head high, she left him to his figures. The brief skirmish had been more of an effort than she had expected. What was it about Jon Roberts that, every time they met, it seemed as if cymbals clashed, the sound ringing discordantly through her body?

CHAPTER FIVE

THE WATERFORD crystal glasses twinkled on the buffet-table. Jon poured himself a glass of sparkling wine and mock-solemnly toasted her. He looked around the room, taking in the details.

'I'm impressed.'

Sophie sipped from her wineglass, hoping she looked more poised than she felt. The formal dining-room, with its rimu-panelled walls, its ornate plaster ceiling-rose and cornices and burgundy velvet curtains and silk hand-knotted rugs from Tabriz, was warmed by the glow from the fire leaping and dancing in the log-size fireplace. The dining-table with its extension could seat twenty, but she had reduced it to half-size. With a chair at either end, the distance was still formidable. It was the gap she needed to keep Jon Roberts in his place.

'There is one item missing, Sophie.'

'Missing?'

'I feel sure you have a candelabrum somewhere.'

Sophie felt her eyes glance towards the cupboard where she had placed the heavy silver sticks.

'I didn't think it was necessary.'

'The romance of the setting definitely demands candles.'

'Not when the people dining are as far apart as

you and I.' Sophie was conscious of his gaze on her, but he turned and helped himself to the tray of hors d'oeuvres, selecting a manzanilla olive.

'Is that a challenge?' He crunched the canapé, his teeth white.

'No, merely a statement.' She hoped her cool answer would not be a further provocation, the man in front of her seemed to regard challenges as personal goals. 'Do try some pâté, it's a Tiromaunga speciality.'

'Gracious, elegant and as cool as the snow queen, the lady of Tiromaunga,' his voice mocked her.

'I'm trying to be civilised. It's difficult in some company,' she retorted, as she went towards the kitchen to check the meal. Away from his intelligent eyes she could relax, expelling a breath of tension. In the oven the blackcurrant sauce had reached the correct consistency on the lamb fillets, and she made an instant decision to serve the dinner. She had made enough small talk with Jon.

On entering the dining-room moments later, the onion velouté in the silver tureen, she saw Jon had reset the dinner plates together.

'Thought I'd do something about the distance between us.' He held out her chair and waited until she was seated before taking the place beside her. 'You didn't really think I'd let you away with such ridiculousness?'

'So long as you understand my feelings.'

'I'll try. Don't worry, Sophie, there's a very long spoon.' Solemnly he handed her the soup ladle. For a brief moment she was tempted to decorate him with the tureen, but his grin disarmed her. Hadn't she decided that she would play the hostess so that her feelings would not be on parade for Jon?

Like children on their best behaviour, they passed dishes, ate, and made polite conversation. Jon had guessed her game, and he was expert at the same tactics. It was only as the meal finished and Jon complimented her on the presentation and taste of the food that she felt he was being sincere. When she began clearing the table he helped her, and once in the kitchen he removed his suit jacket and rolled up his shirt sleeves.

'I guess the least I can do is give you a hand.'

'Thank you.'

Sophie found it hard to continue the pretence while Jon was being helpful. She flicked on the radio to check the weather forecast, and they listened as they tidied the room.

'More snow around the Alps and foothills. Clearing tomorrow,' Jon repeated thoughtfully. 'I wonder what time. I've an important meeting in Christchurch tomorrow afternoon.'

'Do you mean to say the world can go on with its business without you?'

'Not by my choice.' He smiled, then turned back to the radio, listening intently as the list of roads closed was read. 'Still, this afternoon hasn't been a complete waste. I've done an analysis of your business based on your data and future bookings, and it proved our projections accurate. We'll have to give considerable attention to the autumn and summer periods. Incidentally, those ideas you were working on for promotion were rather good. The garden idea could be a winner.'

'You read my notes?' Indignation burned again. 'Those were just private thoughts, possibilities.'

'In that case, you shouldn't have told me to help myself. I have a tendency to read items placed on my desk.'

'It isn't your desk!'

Sophie flung down the cloth, but he merely took it and rinsed it under the tap before putting it back into position.

'You did invite me to use the office.'

There was no answer for the man's urbanity. Fuming, Sophie conceded his point; she had told him to help himself. Jon Roberts believed in taking advantage when it suited him.

'Is it going to be so very difficult learning to live with me?'

'On a score of one to ten, I'd say ten.'

'I've been called that for other things, too.'

'Spare me the details.'

'I will. I don't kiss and tell. So, little blonde Sophie, what are you doing tonight?'

'There's a play on television, and after that I'm going to bed early. Alone,' she added the word quickly.

'Probably a good idea. You look as if you could do with the rest.'

Sophie glared at him, then marched out of the room and along the corridor. She slowed as she reached the usual guest-suite two doors down from her own, then decided against using it for high and mighty Jon Roberts.

Her lips twitched briefly as she recalled the board-lined room jutting off the storeroom, an architectural blunder that in the early days had been utilised by vagrants and strays. It was the room he deserved; she could even toss in a bale of hay for a bed. Her better nature managed to reassert itself and she headed down the west wing to the red suite. Switching on the heating and making up the big bed took only a few moments, then she went to her father's room and removed new pairs of pyjamas and underpants, a clean shirt and another jersey. She put them into the red suite, then walked to the office. Jon looked up at her approach.

'I've put you in the red bedroom. It's two doors along. Also, I've left some clothes out; you may find them helpful.'

'Poor Sophie. It really goes against the grain to be forced into helping me.'

'Can you blame me? You're not exactly my pin-up of the month.'

'I have my fans.'

'But not blondes; I hope one put you in your place.'

'That blasted article! It was meant to be a piece of fun. It's a pity some people have no sense of humour.'

'Humour depends on whether you're being laughed at or with. Generalisations about groups are offensive.'

'I'll remember in future.' His eyes teased. 'Sophie

Wilton: dislikes comments on blondes. Own hair is beautiful, shining white gold.' He paused and for a fraction of time he held her glance. 'You see, I can pay a pretty compliment to a very special blonde.'

'Don't waste your breath. Excuse me, my television programme will start soon.'

From the surprised look on his face Sophie guessed not many had preferred the company of the square box to that of Jon Roberts. Back in the solitary security of the living-room, she flicked the switch. The screen lit and glowed, colours trying dizzily to form patterns and shapes, only the sound true. Switching on the second channel made little difference, so she shut the set off and sank back with a book. The quietness of the house and the absence of the usual night noises of the countryside disturbed her concentration. She put the book down and wandered to the window. Snow was falling, and she could not even see the edge of the veranda in the darkness. Her earlier intention to check the stock in the woolshed was impossible.

Vaguely she remembered family pictures of earlier heavy falls, tales of isolation, roads taking days to clear, and was glad of the local country road equipment. The roadmen would be at work to open the main road to Highway One as soon as possible. There would still be the driveway to the homestead, but even if she had to dig a path herself to allow Jon to leave she would find a way to do it!

The fire sparked and sizzled and she watched it, absently noting that the last log of pine had been wet. An occasional snowflake fell down the chimney, immolating itself instantly. She placed the screen around the fire and walked round the living-rooms, checking all was in order. Switching on the radio, she tuned to the special AA report on road conditions, but they continued to repeat the earlier closures. Warnings broadcast for the area depressed her. She flicked the radio into silence and glanced at the time. Nine o'clock was scarcely bedtime, yet she felt fragile, like an old piece of glass. In her bedroom she could shed the warring feelings which attacked her every time she ran up against Jon.

As she walked towards her bedroom, she hesitated. She did owe him that ridiculous kiss. Perhaps she would be wise to offer it. If he was a gentleman, he would let her off, wouldn't he?

A cynical smile flashed on her face. Jon might know how to act the gentleman, but he certainly was not one. Feeling like a sheep going to the shearing pen, she opened the office door. Jon looked up, a slight frown showing that his concentration had been disturbed, his fingers still on the calculator.

'I'm just going to bed. I'll say goodnight,' she heard herself babble. 'If you want supper, just help yourself. You know where the kitchen is.'

Blue eyes looked into hers with a slight smile, dismissing her. Sophie sighed with relief as she closed the door behind her. The man was human, after all; he had forgotten the wager.

Curled up in bed, Sophie could at last relax and review the day. It would have been memorable without the arrival of Jon, but his appearance had caused an avalanche which had rolled over her units, as well as Harry's farm, altering not only her life, but Harry's and her father's too. It seemed difficult to believe that her cautious, loving father could so quickly make such a decision. Reluctantly she admitted that Jon had won by giving her father a prize he could not resist. Hadn't she known all her life that her father had wanted part of Harry's land? But surely there could have been some way of negotiating with Harry without involving Jon and the units? Why hadn't Harry told them he was thinking of selling? Or had Jon suggested the sale and Harry for some reason decided he was interested? If Jon had been unscrupulous about using spies to ferret out her father's dream, then no doubt he had done the same to Harry. Sophie shook her head tiredly. She had grown up with Harry, she would have sworn that he was happy with his farm and his home, so why had he suddenly wanted to leave?

She snuggled into the pillow and pulled her coverlet around her shoulders, deciding she was too tired to think about the machinations of Jon Roberts. The man was a charmer; hadn't she found herself drawn to him from the beginning? And over the meal, despite the feelings of anger, she had known the attraction between them was constantly there. She felt herself begin to feel sleepy, her body and mind exhausted by the events and tension of the day. Even Jon Roberts wasn't able to keep her from the gentle thoughts of sleep . . .

The thudding in her dream disturbed her, waking her to the realisation that someone was knocking on her door; and as she rolled over to semi-consciousness the small side light flashed into brightness.

'Sophie, it's almost midnight.'

'What?'

Instinctively she shielded her eyes, her lids fluttering like a moth's wings. Darting thoughts of danger; of the storm; of her father lying injured or even worse; of travellers needing assistance passed rapidly through her mind, but one wide-awake glance at her intruder's blue eyes and his almost tender smile reassured her.

'Jon Roberts, what do you think you're doing?' Indignation helped her sit up and glare at her intruder.

'At the moment, looking at you.' To her fury he studied her, then glanced round the room, totally self-assured. 'Relax, Sophie, I'm not here to rape you.' He moved towards the massive chest that had belonged to her great-grandmother. 'A marvellous piece! The basket with the dried flowers on top reminds me of something . . .' He bent, broke off one of the brown star florets and tossed it to her. 'Is it the colour of your eyes?'

'Get out of here!' Sophie tightened her mouth, remembering only too well the allusion to dried flowers. She felt a tension in her body when she saw that his smile had gone, the sapphire-blue in his eyes narrowed to glacial ice.

'There are no snakes, Sophie.'

She heard the words, though they had been said

at a tone a little more than a whisper

'I've come to collect my wager before the time runs out.'

'You've woken me up because of some ridiculous be ?' She hoped she sounded more incensed than she felt. Wasn't attack the best defence? 'Just who do you think you are? This is my bedroom!' His laughter mocked her.

'I'm Jonathon Roberts, new owner of Tiromaunga Lodge among other things. I've fulfilled my part of the wager.'

In a last futile effort she threw a small bed cushion at him. He caught it and walked with it back to the bed.

'Little snow queen. I warned you I never postpone a debt. You chose this arena.'

Calmly he sat on the bed and propped the pillow back into place behind her head. His touch sent a frisson of feeling as he lifted her hair back into place, his hand caressing the side of her throat, up the jawline and across her cheek to trace the shape of her mouth. Sophie pulled away, trying desperately to remember her self-defence lessons from so long ago. Why hadn't she scrambled out of the bed the minute she had realised he was in the room? His breath on her cheek was distracting her, his hands speaking a magic of their own.

'Why don't you kiss me, Sophie?' His voice was a softly taunting, sensuous murmur against her ear. 'It's almost midnight, and I've no intention of releasing you until the debt is paid. If you're not careful I could charge penalty interest, as well.'

His mouth was mere centimetres from her own. Sophie decided that she would have to pay the debt, and the sooner the better. She leaned forward and pursed her lips so that they touched his for a fraction of a second.

'I hardly think that pays the wager, Sophie. That was a petal from a dried flower, not a kiss.'

His hands were stroking her, causing ripples of feeling on her skin, his eyes dwelt on her mouth, as if already shaping her lips. Anger and passion arced through Sophie. He wanted a kiss, well, she would give him one! She would repay his insults of snow queen and dried flowers!

Closing her eyes, she put out her hands and drew his body down to hers. She felt his surprise and wariness as she slipped her arms around him, slowly finding and following the curve of his back, the shape of his shoulder-blades and the taut strength of his powerful neck muscles. Cradling his head, she pulled him gently towards her mouth, her lips moistened by desire.

The kiss darkened as she held him, feeling his surprise change to pleasure as she moved, goading, demanding and exciting him, her body quicksilver to his touch, until her own control was almost lost in an explosion of sensation.

She wanted him to make love to her!

The plan had reversed itself. Her original intention to make him passionate and then reject him with scorn seemed impossible.

The sonorous chimes of the grandfather clock in the hall reminded her of his earlier boast. ' . . . you'll be kissing me before midnight's struck. Just how far you'll go after that . . .'

She was temporarily distracted by the power of his lips as they kissed the nape of her neck. The smooth feel of his flesh brought back the sting of her fury. He had even undressed before he had knocked on her door!

Sophie pushed him away and pulled herself up to a sitting position, still struggling with her feelings as the twelfth chime rang. It took an effort of will to speak crisply.

'Midnight. I believe I have paid the wager. Switch off the light on your way out, Mr Roberts.'

A sudden stillness froze his action in slipping her gown off her shoulder. She could feel the swift beating of his heart and the shocked intake of his breath. She knew he was looking at her, but Sophie did not dare to face him. Apparently totally controlled, she sought to hide her own feelings by stretching to pick up the wooden hairbrush from her cabinet beside the bed and methodically beginning to brush her hair. It seemed a long time before he moved from her bed, as if all his emotions were being tightly pulled back under leash and the effort took all his energy. When she risked a glance, she was moved by the pain on his face. Sensitive to his need, she stretched out her hand, but he was already standing, and striding to the light switch. Without a glance at her, he flicked it off and then strode to the door, slamming it behind him in a movement which rattled the china ornaments on the picture rail.

Sophie felt the brush slide from her suddenly

floppy fingers. The whole of her body began to shake. Emotions of fear, anger and pride warred with a new ache which seemed to come from her core. A groan escaped her and she buried her head in the pillow, unable to cry, unable to express her grief. She thrust her fingers through her hair in pain, willing herself to shut out the moments when for a few seconds in time they had entranced each other.

It had been a few seconds of total joy such as she had never experienced before. She had been so angry with him, but he had carried his own hurt and anger, and she had not seen it until she had peeled back the layers of his emotions in her kiss. The physical attraction had been only a small part of the kiss. Somehow he had poured balm on her own hurts so they no longer mattered; all she had wanted was to give him pleasure, to satisfy him, to let him cherish her, to love her.

It was the kiss between a man and a woman who intuitively recognised each other. And she had destroyed it. Her pride and anger had wanted a victory. She had the same faults as Jon, the need to score. It was a pyrrhic victory.

It was as though she had stood on a delicate new-leaved plant and deliberately crushed it.

She lifted her head from the pillow, her whole body aching with despair and desire. If only she hadn't . . . She pulled herself up short, her eyes sad; it was too late for 'if'.

The hairbrush fell from the bedclothes on to the floor and the noise startled her. Plagued by misery and wakefulness, she tried the radio in an attempt to shut out her thoughts. The announcer's voice listing the road closures did not help. It seemed as if she would be shut in isolation with Jon for days. There was some comfort when the weather office said the wind showed signs of change in the mountains, until she guessed that, with her luck, the new winds would only bring more snow.

Was Jon lying sleepless and tormented in the red suite? Was he wondering if he had imagined those moments of joy? Why couldn't she blame him? Hadn't he entered her bedroom as if he owned her, waking her with callous disregard, laughing at her distress, taunting her for her natural reluctance all because he had won a seemingly impossible wager?

Why hadn't she laughed, admitted and repaid the debt earlier as if it was nothing?

The clock struck once and she tried submerging herself in the bedclothes in an effort to find sleep. Her bed seemed to hold less comfort than a fakir's bed of nails. She flicked off the radio, pulled the bedclothes around her, and determined to rest. The silence served only to orchestrate her thoughts into a concerto of a thousand screaming, vengeful harpies.

She pushed them into the background by concentrating on the thought of her lodge, and the units. What would she do? Would Jon ask her to stay on? Could she face him, let alone work for him?

It would be impossible to avoid him; even with all his interests he would have to spend time setting up the new complex. One thing was certain, there would never be friendship between them.

Again the clock gonged the hour, and she wondered how she had never been disturbed by it in the past. She remembered lying in bed when she was a child and solemnly counting out the hours, enjoying the rich resonance of the sound. It had always seemed such a comforting 'all's well' call. Twisting and turning in an effort to sleep, she heard it strike the half-hour and then the hour again.

At last she gave up and reached for her dressing-gown. Hot milk was supposed to be a panacea, although she had never needed it in the past. Moving quietly, she flitted wraithlike through the silent corridor to the kitchen. Carefully she slid back the cupboard door and painstakingly lifted out the pot, anxious not to make a sound. The milk in the refrigerator was removed just as carefully, and she even took care pouring the milk and in placing the pot gently on the stove to heat.

The sudden gust of wind distracted her and she listened to it hit the side wall, rattling the old window-catch. If the wind changed, the storm would disappear, the roads would be cleared and Jon could leave. The prospect sent her to the kitchen door and she opened it a crack.

Revealed in the shaft of the kitchen light was a white wonderland. Enthralled, she hastily switched on the side garden floodlights, glad they would not disturb the sleeper in the west wing.

The coldness of the snow-frosted air bit into her as she kicked off her slippers and pushed her toes into the dampness of the ever-ready gumboots. She pulled her wrap tighter around her and stepped out into a new world.

The siren inches from her head blasted itself to a full crescendo, briefly dying to scream again in another crescendo, the cacophony shrilling and echoing through all the loudspeakers in the house. For shocked seconds Sophie froze, then burst into action, cursing the automatic security alarm and her own forgetfulness. The remote control was kept just by the door and she reached for it, her fingers fumbling futilely, scrabbling in the fruit bowl which also held an assortment of pencils, papers and keys as the siren continued to scream and wail in accusing repetition.

The control was not there. Her father had been checking the systems the previous day and he could have left the device anywhere . . . Trying to run, she clump-thumped her gumbooted way down the hall, ignoring the sleepy figure who stood yawning by the red suite. Mentally shutting her ears to the loudspeaker, she pushed the master switch to the off position. The cessation of the noise was an immediate miracle.

'I've heard country folk rise early, but this is ridiculous,' Jon began.

'Sorry, I didn't mean to disturb you. Please go back to sleep.'

A glowering look showed he was hardly mollified. Muttering something under his breath, he returned to his room and Sophie heaved a sigh of mixed emotions. It didn't seem fair that, while she had lain sleepless, he had been in deep sleep.

Her nose crinkled as she smelt the first acrid smell of burnt milk. Realisation of the plight of her drink sent her thumping back quickly to the kitchen; the last thing she needed was a blast on the smoke alarm.

As though she had thought it into action the wail began, winding into a high-pitched whistle that set all the dogs to barking again. The control lever was on the mechanism itself set high about the stove and tantalisingly out of reach. She grabbed a chair to stand on, but before she could position it Jon reached past her and the alarm stopped.

'How many more of those things are you going to set off?' Sophie ignored him while she turned off the element and whistled the dogs to silence.

'Excuse me, I'll open the door to let the smell clear.' Her effort at dignity was totally spoiled as he pushed her away.

'Not until you've switched off that blasted security alarm.' He glanced around and then picked up the remote control device by her father's chair. 'It's an automatic reset type, if I'm not mistaken.'

Sophie avoided touching his hand as she took the device from him and dialled in the code releasing the door. The fresh air was like a penetrating blow, sharp pins and needles in her chest each time she inhaled. Despite that, she moved out on to the snow-marked veranda, drawn as much by the desire to remove herself from Jon as by the beauty of the scene.

Set on a glittering white carpet, the deodar cedar at the end of the veranda was a silver Christmas tree. Snow crystals piled thickly on its branches, sparklers twinkling in the slight breeze.

As she watched, the snow slid from an upper branch to cascade on to a lower, it in turn setting off a small avalanche of silverspun light.

Adjusting to the cold, Sophie walked slowly to the end of the veranda, marvelling at the peace and beauty. A sudden gust whipped the snow, flaying it into hysterical movement. It dropped down softly, exhausted, until the next gust sent it into more despairing eddies.

'Beautiful, but treacherous, an appropriate background for Sophie, the snow queen.'

She hadn't heard him approach. His words chilled her more than the cold air. Instinctively she pulled her wrap more closely around her.

He misinterpreted her gesture, his lips a bitter twist. 'Don't worry, three sirens in one night is all I can take.'

Sophie hesitated, wondering if she would ever have the courage to admit how much she regretted her action. The white world around her gave her the answer. She had to make her peace with him.

'I think I deserve that comment. I'm sorry. I wanted to hurt you.' She saw the surprise in his eyes at her honesty. He looked out past her at the covering of white snow.

'You succeeded. I guess, if I'm to be equally honest, I'd have to say I wasn't exactly Sir Lancelot.'

'You were arrogant, brash and conceited. And very rude,' she added.

'And you were a judgemental little snob who wouldn't admit defeat.'

They looked at each other and both smiled, each silently admitting their faults and their attraction. Another of the glittering Christmas tree avalanches of silver snowflakes spun them together.

'A moment in time,' Jon said softly. Her shivering caused him to turn her to the kitchen. 'It's freezing out here, snow queen. Go back and have your milk, or the next pan will need cleaning too.'

The kitchen had chilled, and Sophie shivered as she stepped inside. Jon went to the stove and poured the mug of hot milk. She noted he had wiped down the stove and put the first pan to soak.

'Thank you.'

'In the hotel business you learn to be domesticated.' He looked at her closely. 'You couldn't sleep? Guilty conscience?'

'Watch it. People who are always right lead endangered lives.'

'I'll try to remember.' His smile began in his blue eyes and seemed to warm her as though he was physically holding her. The wind gusted again and they both heard the sound of a heavy pile of snow slide from the roof. She looked up, immediately anxious.

'Don't worry, Sophie. This house of yours has seen a lot more snow in the past. Off with you to your maidenly couch while I'm resolved to behave myself.'

She smiled then turned to walk away, but the heavy drag of her gumboots spoilt her exit. Immediately he was beside her, taking her drink as she kicked the gumboots off and into place and retrieved her slippers.

'Of course, if you require an escort to your bed . . .?'

'I believe I can manage!'

She felt happy that they could be at ease with each other. Even Jon's purchase of the units could hold advantages. He might offer her the position of manager for the units while he was building the complex, but she would have a salary!

The worry of saving every cent for the mortgage was over. It would be up to Jon to take responsibility, and somehow she knew he would enjoy the challenge. Would it be possible Jon would consult her? When would he begin the hotel complex? What time-scale had he formulated? Just how big would the complex become? Might it not be more than a little exciting watching it grow and develop, especially if Jon encouraged his staff to share ideas?

The wind sighed restlessly and she heard more snow slither off the roof. The old house had been equal to the storm, sturdily meeting the challenge. Its chatelaine had handled the situation badly, but at least she had rescued her relationship with Jon from total disaster. They might never again be close, but they could communicate on a friendly level. And it was thanks to their apologies and the snow beauty—a moment in time.

CHAPTER SIX

SOPHIE finished her hot milk and put the empty mug on the cabinet . . .

Her mouth was in a happy, fat cat smile when she woke in the morning. The bedroom was still semi-dark, so she was astounded by the tell-tale figures on the digital clock radio.

Moving over to the windows she pulled the heavy curtains back, lightening the room to grey. Outside, snow mixed with rain to sleet against the glass. It was impossible to see the trees or even a trace of the garden.

'Good morning, slug-abed.' Jon's tone was warm as she entered the kitchen, showered and dressed, a short time later.

'Even the sun's struggling with his blankets,' she retorted with a gesture to the grey window-view. 'I hope you found some food.'

'Plenty. Eggs, bacon, toast, the works. I did think of taking some breakfast into you, but I decided that waking you in the middle of your sleep was too hazardous a risk.'

'You're learning.' She smiled easily. 'Did you hear the weather forecast?'

'They say it will clear, although I have to admit that at the moment it looks as if the wind simply renewed the same conditions. Two o'clock this morning was probably the one time it was clear.'

'It was beautiful,' Sophie recalled. 'I've never seen anything like it.'

Sophie felt his gaze hold her and felt the surge of attraction power between them. She felt the swift rejection when he continued speaking as if uncaring. 'Have your breakfast, then we should try to work out some plan to feed the sheep. At the moment it's impossible.'

Sophie picked up his cue. 'They will be hungry, but they should be all right. There are sheep nuts in the shed once I can get there.'

'OK, so that's one problem solved. I had thought of skiing there. It could be easier than using the tractor. Possibly your father has skis somewhere I could use? Would you show me where they are, and I can be organised if and when we do get a break in the weather. Oh, yes, I need some fishing lines or long cord which I can stretch from the house to the woolshed.' He saw her unspoken query. 'So I can return even if the weather closes in while I'm out there.'

'We'll both go,' Sophie informed him. 'With two of us working together, it will be faster. Besides, I probably know a lot more about feeding stock than you do.'

The toaster popped up two slices of bread as if to emphasise her words, and Jon nodded agreement. Once she had finished and cleared away her break-fast, they went out to the store-room to check the skis and boots. The fishing reels were put beside the gear.

'If there's nothing else, I'll get back to the office and continue work.' Jon glanced again at the window. 'Just keep an eye on the weather in case I miss the change. When I'm working I tend to be rather single-minded.'

'That will be no trouble.' Sophie watched as he went towards the office. She felt her shoulders slump and her smile falter once he shut the door. Was Jon telling her that he didn't want any closeness between them? That, although he had forgiven, he had not forgotten?

It was almost lunchtime when the snow stopped falling. Sophie stepped on to the veranda to check the conditions. The sky still looked heavy, but to the south-west the clouds were less dense.

How long would it take before the snow cleared? Should she take advantage of the short break in the conditions? The knowledge of the hungry stock decided her. It took vital moments to call Jon and to get themselves into the heavy ski gear.

'Make sure that line is securely fastened to the post,' Jon instructed as he took the reel.

Sophie double-checked, then clicked into her skis and pushed off from the veranda-level. The snow was icy on top from the rain, but the sheer bulk of the powder underneath the layer gave a firm surface. It was difficult ski-slipping along, but to have attempted walking would have meant being caught waist-deep at each movement. Sophie followed the line of the back driveway, guided by the occasional tree, the fence posts almost obliterated. The woolshed looked almost glamorous, she decided, under its coat of snow, but the sound of anxious bleats gave her no time to admire the scenery. She shed her skis and helped Jon fasten the cord around the door-handle. Inside, she ran to the pens. Several sets of green eyes looked at her reproachfully, as though blaming her for their conditions. Most were conserving their heat by resting. It took only a few minutes to feed and check the stock.

'That's it?' Jon looked at her and she nodded. 'Let's get going. I think the snow's starting again.'

Her skis were already covered by the layer of snow and she gazed around. There was just enough visibility to see the way, so she was glad of the fractional ground slope which meant they could actually ski back towards the house. Even as they moved towards the rear gate the snow surrounded them, blotting out their path. She could not believe the white curtain which totally obliterated all trace. For a panic-stricken moment she wondered which way was the right one.

'Sophie! Hold on to my hand. I've the cord, remember.' It was slow progress, as Jon was extremely careful not to put any pressure on the line. She did not want to think what would happen if the line snapped. Why hadn't she insisted on their wearing their correct ski clothing? It was so cold, her limbs felt as if she was turning into a snowman. Each breath began to sting her chest. Tales of people lost in blizzards conjured phantoms in the air. She yelped sharply as a ghostly shape brushed wet, trailing fingers across her face.

'What's wrong?' Jon stopped instantly. 'You all right?'

'Of course I am,' she muttered ungraciously, not willing to admit she had been frightened out of her wits by fronds of the kowhai tree. At least she knew exactly where she was. The end of the veranda was only a couple of feet further away. A small grunt told her Jon had hit the pillar before she had a chance to warn him. Scrambling out of their skis, they stopped only long enough to dump them by the kitchen doorway.

'Get inside. It's freezing.'

Sophie didn't need Jon's words to encourage her stiff movements. The warmth greeted them like an old and beloved friend when they entered the kitchen. Sophie found she was shivering, not just with cold and fear, but something else. She hadn't wanted to let go of Jon's hand. Her body began to react to the heat, and she was content just to stand and let the warmth soak into her being.

It was several moments before either of them could summon up strength to talk. She risked a glance at Jon and smiled at the sight.

'Why are you grinning like a smug pug?' He had caught her expression.

'You look like an understudy rehearsing for the part of Worzel Gummidge,' she chuckled. 'He's a scarecrow.'

'I know who he is. You're probably right. For that matter, you don't look ready for a garden party either.' He plucked some snow from her jacket. 'Do you want some help getting out of those boots?'

'I can manage, thanks.'

'In that case I'll go and take a shower. You should, too. It will help warm you.'

Without waiting for her reply, he strode down the corridor to the red suite. Sophie watched him go, a frown on her face. Something had changed. The atmosphere between them had chilled, almost as if he had remembered something or someone . . . She pulled off her own heavy boots and decided he probably had a girl he was missing. The thought weighed her down strangely.

After her shower Sophie went back to the kitchen. She would cook lunch, and in making it something special she could let Jon know she was grateful for his assistance with the stock. Without his insistence on the line they might have been still struggling in the cold. How long could they have lasted?

Shaking her fears and possibilities away, she studied her pantry. Her decision made, she reached for one of the containers holding some of the salmon caught by her father in the nearby Rakaia River. Half an hour later she looked at the table. She had set the kitchen one; it was smaller and more cosy in the room, with the pot-belly fire going in the corner. The salmon she had baked slowly in special miniature fish-shaped dishes using a recipe her mother had prided herself on. Inspecting the dishes carefully, Sophie stopped to call Jon from the office.

Only when she heard the office door shut did she carefully tip the fish out on to the plate. A quick glance to check both were perfect, then she arranged the witloof in petals and spooned on some of her special sauce. She set the plates on the table with a pleased smile.

'Try a Tiromaunga salmon,' she offered.

He needed no second invitation; Sophie began her own meal then relaxed. It was good.

'I didn't know you were such an excellent cook.'

'Something your spies overlooked,' Sophie teased.

'I have always preferred to do my own investigation. Unfortunately it's neither practical nor profitable.' His tone was reserved. Sophie anxiously tried two or three bites more, making sure she hadn't made some horrendous mistake.

'You do eat fish?' she enquired a little hesitantly, wishing she had asked him before she began cooking.

'Yes. This is the equal of meals prepared by my chef at Taupo. He's an authority on the subject.'

She should have felt thrilled with such high praise. Instead she knew something was wrong. She stumbled through her meal, the fish almost choking her. Jon continued to eat and the silence between them grew. Finally she pushed her plate away.

'Jon, at least tell me what is wrong?'

'After lunch we can discuss the matter.'

'I'm not a child.'

He looked at her steadily. 'I'm aware of that. I've spent a lot of time doing analysis, as that was the area of your records that particularly interested me. Consequently, it wasn't until I did a routine budget check this morning that I picked up something unusual. Everything balances, but there is an obvious anomaly.'

'An anomaly? You mean I've made a mistake?' She

frowned. 'I can't think where.'

His eyes seemed to pierce her. 'Sophie, I'm not a fool. I've seen books fiddled by experts.'

'You're saying I've . . . cooked the books?' Sophie was so astounded she could only gape at him, her eyes wide. In the glacial blue gaze that met hers she recovered quickly. 'I am not dishonest. It's possible I've made some small error, but my books all balance. Are you certain of your calculations?

'I am not accustomed to having my mathematical ability questioned,' he spoke crisply.

'You've questioned my honesty,' Sophie blazed back. 'Show me where I'm supposed to have cheated. And who would I cheat? My own father?'

'The Inland Revenue Department. My guess is you've saved yourself at least two and half years' personal income tax. No one could live in this day and age on the amount you are supposed to have paid yourself. According to your records you've earned less in three years that most people would in six months, *ergo* you're not declaring it.'

Staggered, Sophie could only stare at him.

'Quite a few people still pay in cash, don't they?' he continued brutally. 'For the first three months you paid yourself a proper salary, but after that it dropped to pocket money. It wouldn't have kept the women I know in knickers.'

How could she begin to explain that every cent was accurate; that she had taken almost no wages in order to cut down the mortgage?

'You're wrong! The figures are correct . . .'

'Spare me the drama, the tears and the tantrums.

I've seen better actresses than you. What you did hasn't hurt me; in fact discovering it helps me. I know not to offer you employment . . . but I will offer you one piece of advice. Correct the books before an auditor sees them.' Dismissing her, he returned to his meal and forked the last piece of salmon.

'I hope it chokes you!'

Sophie rushed from the room, determined not to let ɹon see the tears in her eyes. In her bedroom she faced up to the shock. How could she prove her innocence?

Her bank balance knew the truth! The inspiration crashed as she realised that Jon would simply laugh at her. He would expect her to have other bank accounts. There was no way she could prove she didn't have more than one.

Eyes hurt with misery, she stared glumly out of the window, absently noting the thickness of the snow piled against walls and trees and fences. The storm had destroyed itself in its last savage blizzard. She watched the sky as the faint blue line became a definite strip, growing wider to belly into a fat curve. The once powerful heavy grey clouds, now emasculated, were being pushed back like feeble old men to the mountains.

Outside a thousand little noises began to reassert themselves. Water gurgled in the guttering as snow melted and sloshed its way from the roof. A blackbird appeared from the stark whiteness of the walnut tree and defiantly chortled its pleasure at the sight of the sun. The triumph of its song was interrupted by a rendering crash, and Sophie gasped as the giant gum split its main branch. The weight of the snow had been too much. She looked anxiously at its mate, but it seemed to be holding up its unusual load.

She could remember helping her parents plant the gum on her fifth birthday. There had been a party to celebrate, and Harry had been invited to plant the second one; he always called it his tree thereafter. He had always been proud that his gum had grown taller and faster and stronger than hers; it had been some time before she had realised they were two different varieties.

She tried not to let the loss of the tree worry her, but it seemed a potent symbol. Bleakly, she looked at her garden, seeing other trees which had lost branches and imagining the devastation down the driveway and around the farm shelterbelts. With something of a shock she realised that she hadn't thought of the units. The snow would be a real test of David's design and the builder's workmanship. If Jon had wanted proof of their quality standard, all he had to do was to put on the skis and check them. Her mouth twisted slightly. He was probably waiting until after the storm to do a full examination.

It seemed strange to think that within a short space of time she would have no interest in them or in the complex Jon proposed. He could stay well out of her way. In fact, she would erect gates barring the access from the units to Tiromaunga.

The sound of a helicopter buzzed faintly in the distance and she watched as it appeared, a large dragonfly gradually growing to its true size. It seemed to be flying straight towards Tiromaunga, and she guessed the pilot was using the dark trees as a point of reference in the snow. Did it look such a magical world from the pilot's view? Was a news team aboard filming the scene for the television news?

'Sophie!'

The sound of her name surprised her. Surely Jon knew she didn't want to see him? Had he realised her distress and decided he had made a grave error of judgement? Her thoughts mashed with the sound of the approaching helicopter, but she went reluctantly to the door and opened it. Jon stood there, dressed in his business suit, looking formal.

'I just came to say goodbye and to thank you for your hospitality.'

'Well, I know I'll be pleased when you leave, but don't you think you are carrying things a little too far? The roads won't . . .'

The noise of the helicopter rotor clacking in time with its engine forced her to stop. Jon pointed upwards and, astonished, she realised his meaning. The helicopter had come to collect him!

The noise grew ever more deafening as they walked down the passage. As he was about to put on the skis Jon said something to her, but with the craft landing on the lawn it was impossible to hear. Sophie watched as he skied out to the craft, removed the skis then climbed aboard. A minute later she received a brief wave of acknowledgement then the craft rose straight up, its ascent causing a minature snowstorm. By the time the snow had settled the noise had softened to a dull drone in the distance. Only the skis remained, an absurd, surrealist picture in the middle of the white lawn.

Feeling strangely abandoned herself, she walked slowly back to the kitchen. Jon's departure had been so sudden, and to her so unexpected. Yet he had been prepared. Without telephone communication, how had he managed it? She gave up on the puzzle and prepared to clean up the lunch-time fiasco. The spotless bench and the table with its accustomed bowl of fruit forced her to admit Jon's claim for domesticity was well-based.

Making herself a cup of tea, she settled in the comfort of an easy chair to try to work out some plan for the following days. How long would she be alone? When would she be able to let the stock out? Could she manage the feed supply in the meantime? She calculated she had enough feed in the shed for two days, and once that was exhausted she would have to fetch more from the barn. Would the snow have melted sufficiently in that time? When would her father return? Would he expect her to drive the tractor over to pick him up? She glanced again at the weather. It seemed to be improving all the time. She could imagine that already workmen would be girding themselves against the cold to restore roads and telephone lines to normal. Jon would be cold in the helicopter dressed only in his suit. She ridiculed herself for her thoughts. A helicopter could be as warm as a car, and what was she doing wasting time thinking about him? He hadn't given a moment's thought to leaving her in snowy isolation with the responsibility of several hundred sheep!

'So much for chivalry,' she muttered aloud. Her

tea finished, she went to the red suite, intending to clear all trace of Jon's visit. Stripping and remaking the bed, dusting and polishing the furniture all took time. She was vacuuming the carpet when the noise of the motor stopped her. As soon as she switched off the vacuum cleaner she realised the sound was increasing, and she identified it immediately. A helicopter? She waited for it to fly past, but instead the sound continued to crescendo. Surely Jon wasn't returning? But why?

Sophie ran down the hall to the front door, opening it just in time to be sprayed by the blast of snow whirred up by the machine. This time a short rope-ladder came from the belly of the craft like an umbilical cord. Climbing rather cautiously down was her father. He reached for the skis they had landed beside, flicked them into position and minutes later he enveloped her in a giant hug. The helicopter began to ascend and again the snow sprayed them, but this time they both laughed.

'Sophie! It's good to be home!' Her father brushed snowflakes from his face and grinned. 'My word, that Jon's a character, isn't he? Talk about special delivery!' He bent to remove the skis, propping them against the front wall. 'Do you know he owns that machine? In fact, he has a fleet of them? Mainly to take his guests into fishing and tramping spots.'

'Really? I'll put the kettle on. Or would you rather have a drink?'

'No need. I had one with Jon and Harry. We had quite a lot to celebrate, and as Jon had his own pilot he didn't have to worry about driving!'

Sophie didn't feel much like smiling, sure in her own mind that Jon wouldn't have bothered to pick up her father without reason. As they walked down to the living-room she voiced her opinion.

'He wanted to meet me again,' her father answered. 'Besides, he pointed out that he hadn't liked leaving you here on your own.'

'I guess I must be more of a suspicious old harridan than I knew,' Sophie admitted. 'I wouldn't have expected him to bother unless he had some ulterior motive.'

'Jon? Don't you like him?' Her father seemed astounded. 'But he's given me the dream of my life! It's a break I'd never have expected to happen. I know it's probably a bad shock for you, Sophie, you always said you enjoyed the work, but since I've had time to think, I believe I made the right decision. The point is they will still be there and Jon's going to be looking for a manager for them. He'll ask you. He couldn't get better. You'll have proper wages again and short hours. You don't really mind too much, do you?'

'Of course I mind!' she exploded, unable to give him meaningless reassurance. Seeing the disappointment on her father's face, she forced herself to silence. She looked away to the snowclad garden, drawing from its quiet. 'It's all right, Dad. I can understand your temptation. I suppose I should say thank you for giving me the chance to run the units.' She struggled to find a smile and was rewarded by her father's hug.

'I'm sorry, love. I will make it up to you one day.

If it wasn't for your efforts there would have been too big a mortgage for me to cope with from Harry's farm. The high interest rates are so much of a burden. As it is, I'll ask to transfer the mortgage. I should have discussed it with Jon.'

'Don't worry about him, Dad. He's quite able to look after his own interests.'

'He helped look after mine. He didn't have to help feed the sheep. He's thoughtful, Sophie. And super-efficient. I'm looking forward to having him stay with us on his routine visits.'

'Dad! What did you say? You didn't invite him here?'

'Yes, of course! But Jon would have none of it unless it was on a proper business footing. He explained that he needed the office and storage areas, plus some room for his staff.' Her father stopped and fished triumphantly in his pocket. 'Here it is, all signed and sealed. One year's lease on the west wing of Tiromaunga, starting from settlement date.'

Sophie could only look aghast at her father. The prospect of having Jon in and out of her home, never knowing when she might run into him, unnerved her.

'The money will be helpful. He offered a very good rental.' Theo saw her dismay. 'I didn't even think about turning him down. You know as well as I do he will need the office and the storage areas, and a room for his staff as well as accommodation for himself.'

Another slithering, sloshing sound on the roof had them both glancing out of the window in time to see a sheet of snow temporarily block the outlook. Seconds later it spilt over on to the veranda and banked itself against the wall.

'There's going to be a mess outside,' Theo commented.

'You're lucky there's not one inside,' Sophie countered. 'Jon Roberts knew I'd never agree to the lease. That's why he went to pick you up. He's a shrewd, cunning Machiavellist!'

'Are you sure you won't come with me to the solicitor's for the settlement today, Sophie? You know the invitation for lunch with Jon was extended to you.'

'Positive.' Sophie straightened her coat. 'Besides, I'm meeting David Alfield for lunch. I think we're ready to go. Oh, is that the mail? Anything interesting?'

'Most of it's for the lodge. I'll take it down to the office. Sorry, Sophie, I really blew your position. I just took it for granted that Jon would ask you to stay on as manageress.'

Sophie's mouth drooped a little. It had hurt badly that morning when she had hung up her keys on the office board.

'At least Jon's selected a pleasant family as staff.' Her father riffled through the mail. 'There's a letter for you.' He handed it to her. 'And a bill for me!'

As her father went down the passage. Sophie glanced at the writing, recognising the sharp vertical strokes immediately. Why was Jon writing to her? Hadn't he done enough? She ripped open the envelope and skimmed through the letter.

> Dear Sophie,
>
> It appears I owe you an apology.
>
> After assessing my staff reports, including your weekly linen count and finding it matches exactly with your bookings, which in turn correlate with the financial columns, I was forced to concede your claim could be correct.
>
> Your father's solicitor has sent me copies of the original mortgage documents preparatory to my agreement to transfer the remaining monies, and with that in front of me I can see the amount and scale of your repayments. The amounts concerned are the complete proof.
>
> I deeply regret my earlier assumption,
>
>   Apologetically yours . . .

The definite signature seemed to make the man visible. Sophie could imagine his feelings at finding he had made a mistake. Rereading the letter she studied his phrases. '. . . was forced to concede . . . the complete proof . . .' She screwed up the letter and threw it into the pot-belly stove. He could keep his formal apology!

A little more than an hour later Sophie and her father drove into the Christchurch car park building and Theo glanced at his watch.

'Just right. I'm due at the solicitor's in fifteen minutes. Sophie, I've been thinking. I talked to the new staff and they have all been through Jon's basic training then completed a further specialist programme. At lunch today I could ask Jon to consider you for training, if you like.'

'Not if you want to live to a ripe old age, Dad. I'm not going to beg Jon Roberts for anything. Don't forget, I've already had a couple of positions offered to me, but I intend to have a break first. I need a holiday.'

'Sophie, I'm sorry.'

She couldn't help contrast her father's sincerity with Jon's apology.

'Dad, I've had a month to get used to the idea. I can understand why you sold. I'm even pleased that it's meant the fulfilment of your dream. Just don't expect me to like Jon Roberts.'

Free of the building, Sophie waved her father a quick farewell and walked briskly into the chill of the winter day. The Cashel Street Mall had its share of shoppers and tourists, but she turned and headed along the riverside lawns, barely disturbing the fat mallard and Avon ducks who slept, beak under wing, one eyelid opening then closing indifferently as she passed. Beside the old stone bridge a tree concealed its branches under pink blossom, a picture of spring delighting her until she remembered Jon's gift of the woodland bulbs and his note. She felt instant anger. Hadn't he done enough without invading her every moment?

'Sophie! I was just coming to meet you.' David linked his arm through hers. 'Do I ask you how you feel, handing over your baby?'

'I'm fine,' she began, then realised David saw through her pretence. 'If you want the truth, I feel like screaming and howling at the same time. I've discovered how mean and nasty and selfish I can be. It's not a flattering picture. If one more person tells me how wonderful Jon Roberts is I shall not be held accountable.'

'I won't call him wonderful.' David grinned. 'But I do find him energetic, knowledgeable, demanding and appreciative. Of course, my opinion could be tinged by the fact that this morning I received some good news.' David smiled happily. 'Meet the new architect for the Tiromaunga complex.'

'Congratulations, David. You'll be thrilled. At least that's one decision where I agree with Jon.'

'If you hadn't approved my sketches for the units in the first place, Jon wouldn't have known I existed. As it was, he flew me up to Auckland and then sent me round his other hotels and lodges before he asked me for my ideas.' He paused to usher her into a restaurant they had been walking towards. 'He's really some man.'

'*Et tu, Brute?*'

David met her ironic smile and then gave his name to the waiter. A table for two was set ready overlooking the River Avon with its still bare willow trees.

'Their meals are as good as yours, Sophie. Incidentally, I meant to ring and tell you how much I enjoyed Harry's send-off last week. His party was a great success. Tiromaunga looked magnificent. You must have worked extremely hard, Sophie.'

'I tried. We wanted everything to be right for Harry. Ideally I would have liked a few more days, but of course he had to leave before the new staff could take over his house.'

'I always thought you two would end up at the altar.'

'That was Dad's idea, too. Love is rarely convenient.'

'So you're a free woman now? How about coming into town one day next week? We could have a meal and go to the theatre.'

'I'll think about it. I don't mean to sound ungracious, but I want to get myself together. We've had a strenuous month.'

'The invitation is there when you're ready, Sophie. You're a very special person.'

'It's not every girl who can claim expertise at digging snow drains and clearing gutters, and don't forget felling branches with a chainsaw!' she twinkled.

'To say nothing of clearing Harry's house, feeding stock and running the lodge at the same time,' David added. 'I have my spies.'

The words spoken with laughter made Sophie feel chilled. Jon Roberts had his spies, too. She wondered how the lunch with her father was progressing. Or had they just finished signing away her lodge in the solicitor's office? Her meal suddenly became hard to swallow and she was glad to let David talk, his enthusiasm for the new project and Jon's other hotels and lodges obvious. They finished the excellent coffee and David glanced at his watch.

'Sophie, I'm sorry, but my time is up. I have to get some notes and queries ready for Jon before he flies out at five. He's not a man you keep waiting.'

'You're learning!' Sophie chuckled, blonde hair dancing. They made their way back to the street corner where they parted and Sophie began the shopping. She finished her list and entered the car park building just at the pre-arranged hour of four o'clock. The lights above the lift told her it was some floors away, so she ignored it and ran lightly up the first, second and third flight. By the time she reached the sixth floor and the correct level she had slowed, but it was the sight of Jon Roberts talking with her father which winded her.

CHAPTER SEVEN

SOPHIE knew gratitude for the unknown designer who had placed the stair access at a different angle from the liftwell. She paused to recover her breath, wondering if she should retrace some of her steps. But why should she let Jon bother her? Tossing her blonde hair back, she stepped out to meet them.

'Good afternoon. Everything settled?' Her voice, coolly modulated, sounded completely under control.

'Naturally.' It was Jon who answered her. 'I regret you couldn't join us for lunch.'

Sophie stiffened as his blue eys searched her face. 'I had made other arrangements.'

'I wanted to talk to you in slightly more pleasant surroundings.' He gestured to the grey functional building and the rows of cars.

'There's nothing we have to say to each other.' She even managed a smile. 'Dad, have you the keys? Open my side, will you?'

Jon did not accept the dismissal. 'According to my staff, you have handed over the units in first-class order. I wished to thank you for the co-operation you've given them.'

'It's easy to be helpful to pleasant people.' She saw his eyes flash and his mouth twitch, clearly realising that he himself was not in such a category. He nodded and turned to smile at her father who had just finished unlocking the car.

'Goodbye, Theo.' He shook her father's hand, then looked at Sophie. 'I'll look forward to our next meeting.'

Jon strode to the lift and Sophie gritted her teeth, as it opened just as he reached it. She threw her parcels on to the rear seat, wishing she was aiming them at Jon.

'What a man!'

Her father was developing into a lead singer where praising Jon was concerned, she thought savagely.

'I've just spent one of the best afternoons in my life. He reminds me of that Chinese expression: a machine can do the work of fifty men, but no machine can do the work of one extraordinary man.'

'Forgive my lack of enthusiasm.'

'Why don't you like Jon? I thought it was courteous of him to thank you in person. He put himself out considerably to do that.'

Sophie hesitated. Earlier she had been too hurt to even talk with her father about Jon's accusation. If she told him, the knowledge would only burst his balloon of happiness. A car pulling out of its space suddenly saved her.

'Watch out, Dad. You're not in the ten-acre field now,' she evaded. Her father was kept busy negotiating the car park, and to her relief he had forgotten his question by the time they reached the open road. Over an hour later he slowed the car to turn into the driveway to Tiromaunga, and a happy smile shone on his face as he looked at the well-proportioned historic homestead.

'We've done it, Sophie. Today's work means the old lady should be safe for at least another couple of generations.'

'I'm pleased you have your dream, Dad. I'd better get busy. I rang some of your old friends to help you celebrate. They'll be here at eight.'

'Really? That's great. Who's coming?'

'Nearly everyone I invited. They know how much today meant to you, Dad. The only newcomers are the lodge staff. I thought it would give them a further chance to know some of the neighbours.'

'I don't suppose you invited Jon?' Her father saw her face. 'Sorry I mentioned him. He really is courteous to me.'

Sophie resisted the temptation to be cynical about Jon's good manners. Jon would have made a point of finding out the extent of her father's influence in the local community. Theo Wilton and David's father had been alternating the post of chairman of the area council for years . . . If there were any planning difficulties with the area council zone restrictions or building limits, they were the men whom others would respect. Was that the reason why Jon had made sure his deal with Theo Wilton had been faultless? Sophie drew in a chilling breath as she thought of her father's best friend. Had Jon considered the position of David's father when he selected David as the architect?

Just how big did Jon envisage the complex? Why had he needed so much land? Wouldn't he manipulate and charm people to get what he wanted? Did he intend to use her father? David's father? As the car was driven into the garage, Sophie pushed the problem of Jon temporarily from her mind. There was a lot to fix before that evening's supper.

Hours later, Sophie looked around the living-room with a tired sigh. The party had been a winner from the beginning; her father, on top form, had regaled his friends with tantalising word pictures of the proposed complex and the abilities of the new owner. Sneaking a look at her watch, she was not surprised to see the hands almost touching midnight. She hoped the guests would depart soon; the day had been long. Her alarm had woken her at six a.m.

Sophie had been determined to leave the units immaculate for the new staff and, although they had spent a week there, she had suggested they take advantage of her last day to sleep in. With a full house of skiers she had worked extra hard to complete the task before they came on duty. Placing her unit keys on the office board had been difficult, and she had been glad the room had been empty.

From the hall passage came the striking of the grandfather clock. She felt pain remembering another midnight moment.

'Hold it, everyone! Could I have your attention for a moment?' Theo Wilton waved his glass. 'I'd like you to help me sing "Happy Birthday" to my daughter, Sophie. She's the one whom we should really thank. It was her imagination and work which brought the Tiromaunga units to the attention of Jon Roberts in the first place. So here's a toast to Sophie.'

Amid happy banter Sophie received her song and

good wishes. As the song died down, she saw several had remembered her birthday and she was delighted by their gifts. Her father handed her a package proudly, and when she undid it she saw he had adapted his grandfather's gold watch chain as a necklace for her. Enchanted, she slipped it on. Only then did she see another parcel in her father's hand.

'Jon asked me to give you this, Sophie. He particularly suggested that you receive it as near twelve as possible.'

Conscious of many eyes Sophie could only unwrap the gift, revealing a small, gold clock. Nothing could stop her gasp of pleasure. The clock was the most beautiful she had ever seen. With its face enamelled with spring flowers, the exquisite detail and high quality of workmanship set it apart. The hands of gold showed just past midnight. Carefully she set it on the mantelshelf for all to admire. Only then did she realise no card accompanied the gift. The clock carried its own message.

Made aware of the time, the guests began to drift away, and not much later Sophie heard her father lock the door after the last stragglers. The setting of the outside alarm reminded her of another moment when she had sought Jon's understanding. Then he had not only forgiven her but admired her honesty and admitted his own fault. The immaculate beauty of the snow-covered garden had seemed like a new beginning . . . a moment in time.

Was Jon asking her to accept his apology with similar generosity? Or was he buying her? Should she send the gift back? She went to the clock and picked it up. After studying it, she carefully slipped off the back plate and the inscription was revealed.

'Sophie. To a moment in time. Jon.'

Stunned by the parallel of their thoughts, she replaced the plate and set the clock back on to the shelf. She did not want to forgive Jon. Wasn't the clock typical of his charm? How much did it mean? As she prepared for bed, she tossed the problem around. Her face twisted into a tired smile; the man was developing a habit of sending her gifts she found it difficult to refuse. Despite her earlier weariness she found herself lying sleepless, planning possible answers, and when the old clock struck two she gave up. Jon had a positive genius for disrupting her sleep!

She pulled on her dressing-gown and sat down to write.

Dear Jon,

I find it difficult but I cannot accept your gift. The clock is beautiful, I have never seen one I like so well.

When I saw it I remembered another moment and realised the clock was its own messenger.

Perhaps in time, say about ten years from now, I might feel more understanding; you might like to offer it to me then?

Her decision made, she read the note through, yawned tiredly and crept into bed. In the morning she woke at her usual time, but with the realisation that she didn't have to get up she turned over gratefully and slept again. When she did rise she read the letter over again, decided it said enough and reluctantly began to pack up the little clock. The thought of its delicate beauty being smashed in the post made her hesitate. Jon would be visiting the site in the future. She would put it in the office for him when he was due.

After amending the letter, she unwrapped the clock and took it to her bedroom. It looked good sitting on top of the chest next to the dried flowers. She glanced again at the arrangement. They had served their purpose. Already the first snowdrops and anemones had begun brightening the gardens. On impulse she ran out to the driveway, returning with the first three cream flowers of the Earlicheer bulbs and a couple of dark green leaves. Tossing the dried ones away, she deftly arranged the fragrant delicate flowers in a small vase. Once they were in place, she stood back to check and smiled when she saw how perfectly the clock matched the arrangement. She could only hope Jon wouldn't come too soon!

Absently she looked out of the window, noticing the snow on the mountains. The rest of the day stretched in front of her. There was nothing she had to do. The thought seemed shocking. Again her glance wandered to the mountains and then checked the clear, cloud-free sky.

'I'm off skiing, Dad,' she informed her father as she gathered her gear a short time later.

'Excellent idea.' He nodded approvingly. 'Have a good time!'

As the days drifted by Sophie began to unwind, her body toning as the constant skiing increased her fitness. Most mornings she helped her father for an hour or two with the lambing, then rushed through the housework to spend the rest of the day with friends on the mountain. She was almost glad when the occasional wet day gave her time to sleep and catch up on household tasks. It seemed surprising, but she hardly had time to miss the units.

'Do you know, Dad, it's three weeks since settlement day,' she admitted one morning at breakfast.

'Everything has to be perfect in the units today—Jon's coming.' Theo Wilton smiled at Sophie. 'It's the staff's first inspection.'

'I'm sure all is under control.' Sophie was surprised her voice sounded normal. The mention of Jon's imminent visit had quickly decided her plans for the day. 'I'm heading up the mountain once I've finished checking the stock. Looks like a perfect day for skiing.'

'Leave the sheep to me. Get up the hill early for a change.'

'Are you sure, Dad? I've had such a lazy time lately . . .'

'You needed the rest. Now you're looking tanned and fit.'

'Don't say I told you so!' Sophie grinned. 'Lunch is in the refrigerator.'

An hour later Sophie clicked her boot clamps into place and glanced round the ski field. The sun was shining and in the clear mountain air the spring snow glistened, pristine and inviting. One of the first skiers on the field, she had enjoyed her ride up the chair-lift, despite the morning chill. The trails lay groomed, curving their way down the mountain to the Mount Hutt buildings, and far below Sophie could see the cars and buses moving ever upward. As she gazed around, the whole world seemed to be stretched before her, mountains dropping to the plains, silver lace rivers leading to the ocean, blue horizon meeting blue sky.

The sound of others approaching her lookout made her realise her solitude was over. She looked again at the trail, then, having chosen her path, she leapt into action, skis biting into the snow, sliding, turning, jumping, movements smooth and rhythmical. Exhilarated, she slowed as she approached the lower chair-lift queue area, face tingling, breathing rapid, eyes clear brown sparkles of joy.

'That was some run, Sophie.'

The shock of hearing and seeing Jon Roberts was total. He manoeuvred his skis to stand beside her in the short line.

'The staff were expecting you,' she finally managed.

'I've left my lodge manager to do the inspection. Snow like this was too tempting. Shall we go?'

Their turn at the lift had arrived and Sophie moved up automatically, realising as he lowered the chair's bar that they were trapped together, the lift swinging them high towards the peaks. She risked a glance at him, wondering if he had been waiting for her at the lift queue, but his expression meeting hers was hidden by the dark ski glasses.

'I'm surprised you can take the time off to go skiing,' Sophie accused.

'Don't worry, I'm working. This is called market research. I have to find out the best features of the area before I approve themes for a year-round advertising campaign. Why should I let my staff have all the fun?' He raised the bar as they came to the top and glanced at her. 'Ready?'

Sophie nodded and pushed herself off. She led the way, adjusting her poles as she skied to the start. If Jon intended to ski beside her then he would have to work for it, she thought with a trace of a grin. About to ski off, she felt her arm gripped, forcing her to a halt.

'Let's make it an official challenge.' Despite her own dark glasses, he had read her mind. 'Sophie, if I beat you to the base, you have to help me with some of my market research today.'

Sophie wished she knew just how good Jon was at skiing. His expensive ski gear could be just a rich man's toy, or they could mean he was a mountain ace. His physique was that of a sportsman, but was he a skier? She was on home territory, she knew it as well as the gardens at Tiromaunga, and since losing her lodge she had spent a lot of time on the mountain regaining her skills and fitness. Could she win? The lift clanged behind them and she knew her time was up.

'If I win, then you go your way and I mine.'

'Just for today,' Jon qualified.

The run was clear, they looked at each other and Sophie was off even as Jon nodded. Skis parallel, she forced herself faster and faster, lowering her body, tucking into the curves, determined to win. She had to beat Jon.

She could hear the shush of his skis behind her,

pressing her at every corner. Gradually she began pulling away from him. Counterbalancing, she diverted swiftly to pass another skier, then flashing forward, heart pounding, she skied along a smooth, almost straight section. Almost immediately she could hear the sound of Jon's skis as his longer, powerful legs took advantage of the terrain. He was too close!

Changing her mind about her route, she deliberately let him edge ahead and then pass so he could not follow her plan to use the spectacular jump she had noted on her earlier run. As she approached the spot she straightened to lower her speed, then readied herself for the thrill as she lifted into the air and dropped in long, hovering seconds bending to a smooth, graceful landing on the lower ground. Legs, knees and hips pumping like shock absorbers, she swept on, taking the curves fast, streamlining her body for every possible second, intensifying her alertness to dodge an occasional skier. Down to the last, long straight, the wind stinging her face, her breath sharp rasps, triumph in sight. She risked a glance behind her and saw Jon start his final run at the top of the poma field. She was at least half a minute ahead.

Victory would be sweet.

Too late she saw the ski school, a long line intent on managing their awkward appendages as they streamed after their instructor. Frantic, Sophie slowed, jumped sideways to avoid one, sidestepped another, but the third tried to dodge and lost control, the tips of his skis just catching Sophie's and sending them both crashing. Amid a flurry of snow and abject apology she reassured herself that the learner was not hurt, then climbed back to retrieve her poles. As she checked her bindings she heard Jon's chuckle in the wind as he passed her. Reluctantly she skied towards the queue area, knowing Jon had won.

'Ever heard the tale of the hare and the tortoise?' he grinned smugly.

'A long time ago,' Sophie admitted. 'You ski well.'

'I'm not in your class. Half-way through the race I remembered that the biography on you said you'd represented the area as a teenager.'

Sophie's brown eyes widened. His spies had been thorough. The reminder chilled her.

'Are you all right?' His concern was immediate. 'Did you get hurt?'

'I'm fine.' She spoke quickly and moved away to avoid his outstretched hand. To be impervious to Jon's charm was hard enough, but the physical attraction between them was too strong to tempt. Hadn't she already found out he was dangerous?

'Would you like some coffee, Sophie?'

'No, thanks. Later, perhaps.'

'You're shutting me out, Sophie.' There was a warning in his voice. He reached forward and raised her glasses, so she was forced to look at him. 'I know you.'

'No, you don't.' Her denial was too swift, and she saw the smile on his mouth and the white gleam of his teeth.

'Not as much as I would like to, I'll agree there.'

'Why bother?'

'I'm not sure. You intrigued me from the first moment I saw your photograph.'

'My photo?'

'Yes, there were photos included in the original reports. There was one of you in a garden, and something about you appealed.'

'So you marched right in and smashed everything.'

'Is that how it appears to you?' He studied her. 'You're as fit as a boxing champion, and for my money twice as dangerous. You have a remarkable ability to penetrate my guard. I find myself wondering what you would think and what you would do . . . It's partly those brown eyes of yours; they slash mere mortal men at forty paces when you're angry . . .'

'What is this? The latest in long lines?' Sophie could not let him continue. His voice had dropped to a low murmur and it was wreaking havoc with her intentions to remain cool. 'I'm sure you have more than enough fish to play with already.'

'Fishermen will tell you it's the one who is the most difficult to catch who provides the greatest challenge.'

'A challenge?' Sophie looked at him in furious disgust. 'That's all it is to you. A game you have to win. You don't care about the emotional shocks you inflict. Well, I'm not playing your game, Jon Roberts.' Sophie took off her skis and planted them against a nearby rack, her vigorous movements emphasising her feelings. 'And I never will!'

Five minutes later Sophie sat in the cafeteria, hands wrapped around her mug of hot coffee, her feelings still churning as she viewed the field. Jon had not followed her or insisted on her company. What was the matter with her? Why had she reacted so strongly? Sighing, she pushed her glasses back and then bent to open the top clamp on her boots.

'More coffee, Sophie?' Jon sat down beside her.

'Only if I'm allowed to throw it at you.'

'You're over-reacting.' His tone was maddeningly calm.

'I thought you'd given up.'

'That would have been out of character, don't you think? I've been insulted before. In comparison you have the proficiency of a beginner.' His smile was twisted as he glanced at her. 'A promising beginner, I'll admit.'

'I'm sure if I stay in your company for very long I'll become a specialist.'

'All right, Sophie, let's stop this right now. I know I upset you when I bought the lodge, but you were beginning to accept that.' His blue eyes seemed to shadow as he looked at her. 'There was a very special moment when we both understood each other. Remember, Sophie?'

'I remember.' She turned her head to avert her gaze, but his silence forced her to look back at him.

'Sophie, I'm not very good with apologies. I am sorry I thought you were a cheat.'

'It hurt,' she could only mumble.

'Me, too.'

Sophie looked at him, surprised.

'Listen, my little snow queen, I knew from the beginning, from the moments of the first photo, that I was attracted to you. There you were in your garden, and I remember thinking you could be a source of—shall we call it temporary gratification? I think I'd had some preconceived idea of a spoiled, rich, blonde socialite who had grown up in a background of wealth. My reports portrayed you quite differently; in fact they made you out to be such a paragon that I told the authors I didn't pay for writing fantasy. When I met you I began to see their reasoning. Even when I was rude and you were very angry, you were able to handle the situation. In fact, you earned my respect.'

'It didn't stop you from buying the site.'

'Of course not.'

'Business comes first?'

'I've achieved a lot the past twelve years. No pain, no gain.'

'But in the case of the lodge it was *my* pain.'

'It wasn't meant to turn out that way.' Jon reached out to touch her hand. 'I'd thought you were a very special person, so it was a shock when I found the supposed discrepancy. There you were, driving me crazy each time you moved, looking at me with your brown eyes anxious, demanding to know what was wrong . . .'

'I got both barrels,' Sophie supplied.

'Yes. Much later, when I saw the reports and the rest of the information, I knew you'd been speaking the truth. I tried to write but . . .' He shrugged his shoulders. 'I wasn't prepared to be honest with myself. I hoped the clock would help. I was sure you'd realise . . .'

'A moment in time?' Sophie said softly.

'Have you any idea how beautiful you are, Sophie?' Jon said quietly, his eyes sincere. Sophie felt his gaze travel slowly over her to rest on her mouth in a charge of sensuality which sent the blood coursing through her body. As though he was unable to resist touching her, he reached out his hand and gently traced the strand of blonde hair which had curled its way from her protective hood. His touch produced wavelets of feeling which rippled through her.

'When we make love, Sophie——' he paused and his voice became even more gentle and deep '—it's going to be as great as those mountains.'

Sophie caught her breath, forcing herself to ignore her body's response. 'You're going too fast for me, Jon.'

'What do you want, Sophie?'

She thought for a moment. 'The same as everyone else, I suppose. Love and marriage, a commitment to one person, later a family.'

Jon seemed taken aback. 'You play for high stakes, Sophie.'

'You asked what I wanted. I didn't mean you were necessarily the right person. That's my whole point. We hardly know each other, Jon. When we do meet, it's nearly always to clash.'

'Like a pair of cymbals!' he agreed, as he took her hand again. 'There's more than air in vibration between us.'

A group of skiers jostling to reach the next table interrupted their privacy. Jon stood up. 'Come on, Sophie. Let's just see if we can spend the day together and take it from there.'

Sophie nodded and followed Jon to the crowded field. They made their way slowly through the queues to the top chair.

'Do you know you have the softest, most enchanting lips I think I've ever seen?' he murmured, as the lift swung them upwards. He bent and dropped a snowflake kiss on her mouth. 'I have to seize my chance when I can, Sophie; right now I know you can't get away.'

He took off her sunglasses, pocketed them, then slipped one arm along the back of the chair, drawing her close. His lips torched her response, enkindling her entire body. She felt a dizzying ecstasy engulf her. It was a shock when Jon drew back as the ride finished. They were both silent, but stunned by their reactions. Near the top of the South Peak they drew aside from the trail to regain their balance.

Together they looked at the incredible scene; range upon range of mountains against the backdrop of the sky, the sun highlighting the area immediately around them, soft white snow on sheer black rocks. Sharing it with Jon, Sophie had never seen its magnificence with such clarity, but the contrasts were sharper, the peaks more hostile and the dangers more evident. It took an effort of her will to break from Jon and gesture to the trail.

'Let's go!'

Knowing that Jon would appreciate a challenge,

she led the way, deliberately selecting a route full of twists and turns. When they slowed for one exceedingly sharp patch, she heard his chuckle.

'If I break my leg you have to nurse me, Sophie!'

'I'm not worried, you'd be more likely to twist your knee ligaments.'

'And to think I thought you had a soft heart.'

She selected another slightly easier slope to finish the run; the last thing she needed was Jon's stay at Tiromaunga to be protracted!

'That was great. You can see why this place is called "the ski field in the sky". How high were we?'

'More than two thousand metres.'

'It was great, much more fun than working out in a gym!' he laughed. 'Come on, this time I want to make the run along the top of the ridge.' He pointed it out.

'The virgin mile,' Sophie supplied the trail's name automatically, then realised from his grin that he had known all along.

Before the day was finished they had explored a number of different trails, each one a fresh challenge. Sophie pulled off her ski hat with a tug after one long run from the top to the base field at four and a half thousand feet.

'I'm exhausted!' She pushed her glasses back against her blonde hair.

'The chair-lift will be stopping soon. We'd better go up to the first lift, then ski down to the car park. Think you can make it?' Something in his innocent voice made Sophie move just in time. The snowball he had thrown splattered on to the rock beside her.

She gathered some snow and heaved it after him, but he had retreated to the lift with remarkable speed. As she caught up to him near the last small queue, he studied her intently.

'Do you realise that you still haven't shown me the place where you managed to leap ahead?'

'You noticed? What a shame it's too late now!' She smiled cheekily. 'With you, I need all the aces I can hold.'

'Why bother?'

He had stopped her progress by the simple expedient of putting out his pole. Surprised, she turned to look at him, and something in his attitude caused her body to sing.

'Don't you know you hold the joker?' His words were very quiet.

'I don't understand.'

'You mean you don't want to acknowledge what has happened.' He spoke roughly. 'Don't tell me you didn't feel the physical force when we kissed. I was there.' His hand reached out and touched her face, and she felt the quick tremble shiver through her. His lips smiled slightly and she knew he had observed her reaction.

'Just chemistry,' she managed, determined to keep the atmosphere between them on a light-hearted note. She skied to join the queue and he followed her and took her hand, deliberately pulling off her glove to count.

'I would have said biology myself, or perhaps simple maths. One and one make two.'

Sharing the triple chair-lift meant the conver-

sation changed, to Sophie's relief. She wasn't ready
to admit anything to Jon. It was only as they were
driving into the gates of Tiromaunga that she could
admit to herself she had wanted the afternoon to last
for ever.

CHAPTER EIGHT

'SOPHIE, I'd like to take you out for a meal tonight. I'll have to do two hours' work first, but I'll be ready a little before eight. Will you arrange for a table? Perhaps in Ashburton?'

'I think I'll be able to do that much.' She smiled. 'You take a lot for granted. Who said I'll go?'

'The wager, remember?' Jon's blue eyes gleamed. 'But this time I think you'd go with me, regardless.'

'You're right, of course,' she said happily as she parked the car. She almost steered the four-wheel drive through the garage when Jon leaned over and dropped another of his magical feather-touch kisses on her mouth. Instinct made her brake, and she switched the engine off hastily when John put his arm around her to turn her to face him.

'Just as well you didn't do that on the mountain road.' She tried to sound severe. 'We could have fallen hundreds of feet.'

'It was a temptation, but I managed to resist. I have a stong desire . . . to live.' His hand traced the outline of her face, his fingers gentle as they followed the curve of her lips, finally resting on the centre. As though he had marked the spot, he dropped another brief kiss on her mouth, then his lips touched hers again, settling possessively, masterfully wreaking cataclysmic havoc with all her determination. Abandoning herself to the sensual pleasure of being in his arms, answering the swift demands of his touch, aware of the scent of his aftershave, the hard warmth of his body, she melted into ecstasy.

The sudden sounding of the horn when she moved her arm shocked her to sanity. Wide-eyed, she looked at Jon, his face an inch from her own.

'You drive me crazy, Sophie,' he murmured. 'That blasted ski suit . . .'

'Just as well it's protecting me. I'm finding I have few defences where you're concerned, Jon.'

He sat back and pushed one hand through his hair ruefully. 'They might be few, but I'm finding them effective.' As he leaned back Sophie rested against him, feeling cosseted when he slipped his arms around her. Gently she intertwined her fingers with his.

'Mmm. It's nice just sitting here with you. I never thought of a garage as being a romantic place before!'

'Unfortunately we've got to move. I've two hours' work ahead of me.' He dropped another teasing kiss on her ear and nuzzled her. 'But we have the night and all tomorrow.'

'And after that? Where will you go?'

'Auckland for a week, then I've a lecture to deliver to a travel agents' conference in Sydney, and while I'm there I want to arrange the marketing of another holiday plan. After three days I fly back to Auckland and begin my routine six-monthly inspections. That will take another three weeks, then it will be down here for a couple of days to meet the local area council and discuss the preliminary plans . . .'

'That means I won't see you for at least a month!' Sophie said in dismay. Jon Roberts was not a man who needed encouragement. His touch sent the whole of her emotions into outer space for the length of the kiss. At last they were silent, only able to hold each other. Sophie felt a tremble shiver through her. Jon spoke again.

'I've arranged to base myself here for a few months once I've finished the inspections. It will be easier than flying down weekly while the complex is under construction.'

'That sounds logical.' Sophie could not keep her voice free from the excitement she felt. 'Your computers and fax machines can keep you in touch with the other places.' She paused at a sudden thought. 'Where's your home?'

'I have an apartment at the Kingdom in Auckland. As well I've a suite at my Taupo Lodge.' He stopped at her expression. 'Why the frown?'

'I meant where you grew up, your parents, your family?'

'Not everyone has a place like Tiromaunga to call home.' He checked his watch. 'Sorry, Sophie, but you'll have to excuse me. I'm expecting a call from San Francisco, and I said I'd be available at five-thirty.'

Sophie saw he was smiling, but she had felt the tension in him. He kissed her briefly and opened the door. The rasp of her skis as he lifted them off the rack seemed to echo the tearing of her heart. She watched him go across the lawn, his skis against his shoulder like a cross. Whatever his past, he was not ready to share it with her. Thoughtfully, she put away her equipment in the rear storage area and then went into the house, conscious of her own heritage of love.

Dressed to go out, Sophie checked her appearance in the mirror carefully. She had pulled her hair back from her face and rolled it into a soft halo effect very different from her perky side ponytail or her severe ballerina plait. Gently she pushed it, but the pins held securely. Satisfied, she glanced at the soft pink woollen sweater dress she had bought to wear at Harry's farewell. From the number of compliments she had received on that occasion, she knew the dress highlighted her colouring. She wanted to look her best. The gold chain shone softly as she fastened it into position around the neckline.

The whirring of the grandfather clock as it prepared to strike reminded her Jon would be waiting. She went out to the living-room, where her father glanced at her.

'You sure took a long time to get ready,' he grinned, 'considering you're going out with someone you can't stand.'

'That was this morning, Theo.' Jon had entered the room and his eyes rewarded Sophie for her trouble. 'Sophie, you are beautiful.'

'Thank you, Jon.' She forestalled her father's

lecture on driving by giving him a quick kiss on the cheek. 'We won't be late, Dad. Goodnight.'

It took them little time to drive to Ashburton where the restaurant proprietor, recognising Sophie, welcomed them with pleasure. In the fireplace large logs flamed, the fire leaping and dancing in the dozens of reflections on silver and glassware, the damask tablecloths and serviettes adding to the feeling of graciousness. Their table was set in a window alcove, giving them privacy. From the beginning to the end of the artistically presented and well-cooked meal, Jon was a charming host. Everything seemed perfect, but Sophie was perturbed by the way Jon blocked every question to his past like a superb test cricketer. He diverted attention so easily that she began to wonder if it was her imagination. Even when she spoke of skiing and other general matters, he still seemed not as relaxed as he had been in the afternoon. Her memory of another meal which had ended disastrously held back her enquiry, but as they received their coffee she put her hand out to him.

'Something's worrying you, isn't it? This time I know it's not something I've done, but is it something I could help with?'

'How is it you can read me so well?' Jon gave a wry smile. 'With you, I find it difficult to dissemble.' He paused and looked at her. 'My advertising team has struck a problem with the draft marketing scheme. The truth is, I should have flown back tonight. Instead I wanted to be with you.'

'I should be flattered.'

'Yes, you should.' He smiled. 'My secretary was surprised when I told her to cancel the tickets she'd ordered for me. She knows business always comes first.' He shrugged his shoulders. 'At least it did until a certain brown-eyed, blonde-haired woman called Sophie Wilton began to fascinate me.'

'There's hope for you yet,' Sophie teased.

'That's what my secretary said. She thinks I live only for ambition.'

'Is she right?'

'I usually find her accurate.' He put his cup down and Sophie was aware of him searching for an explanation. 'I like a challenge. Ambition grows. Look at a baby, he reaches out for something and struggles to move until he achieves it. Temporarily he is satisfied, until he sees something brighter and he learns to crawl to it, so he can take it. Successful, he wants something else, better or bigger. He stands, walks, runs. He tries bikes, cars, planes. With every plateau reached there are new horizons.'

'And that satisfies you?' She felt a chill at such a philosophy.

'I like the challenge and the rewards. Early on I decided money was the key and I determined to make a great deal, and as I'd more or less grown up in hotels it seemed to be the logical way for me.' He stopped abruptly. 'But I'm breaking one of my own rules. I should kiss you on the lobes of your pretty pink ears, but in the meantime . . .'

Sophie felt his touch on her hand as he picked it up, turned it over and dropped a kiss in her palm sealing it with her fingers. The gesture was enough to send her pulse-beats into rapid time, and she could feel the drum-beat echo in him as her hand rested against his jaw and neck. Completely distracted, she did not realise until a little later that Jon had again avoided talking of his family. Was that the rule he had mentioned? Her brain sorted out the facts like a computer scrolling different scenes and impressions before her. She remembered calling him a robot because he seemed incapable of caring feelings. Was there a link between his family and his control of his emotions? By some twist, was she falling in love with half a man? A man incapable of loving someone else, a man who saw pleasure with a woman as another brief challenge?

Yet could she deny the intensity of their physical attraction? Did she want to? She remembered his phrase '. . . a source of temporary gratification'. The comment came back to her with the taste of bitterness. Had those who had tried to love him been used then tossed aside like the wrappings round takeaway food?'

'You're very quiet, Sophie.'

'Thinking about you.'

'I can only commend your choice of subject. But I knew you were a woman of taste!' He caressed her with his eyes. 'Your hair looks like fine threads of gold, Sophie. I approve.'

'It took longer, but I wanted to look my best for you,' she admitted. Gently she touched his lips with her fingers. 'I like compliments, but that one was intended as a diversion. You used it to escape talking about yourself.' A twist to his lips acknowledged her accuracy. Encouraged by his silence, she spoke softly. 'Jon, I want to know more about you. You have probably read nearly all about me thanks to your reports, but I have only,' she paused and thought, 'an ABC about you. An able administrator, brilliant businessman, and for "c" you have the charm of a conman—but that's only the first three letters of the alphabet.'

'I think that's a good start.' He smiled. 'My staff sometimes call me the demanding dictator . . . then we could add energetic executive, but "f" . . .' His smile disappeared.

'Family?'

'No.' The denial was as sharp as a diamond needle.

'No family? I don't understand.'

'My father and my older brother were killed in a road accident when I was thirteen. It was my fault. I ran on to the road. A car swerved to avoid me and went out of control.' He looked at her with sudden anger. 'And don't give me that "I'm sorry" rubbish. It doesn't mean a damn thing to you, and why should it?'

She ached to hold him, to comfort him with her compassion, but his emotion told her he could not accept sympathy.

'You're right. Their deaths mean little to me. But it does affect me because it obviously hurts you. I think the accident probably ripped you apart, too, and the anger and the grief are still bleeding.'

'Don't come the psychologist!'

'It might help you to talk to one if you can't talk to your friends.' Sophie saw the bleakness in his eyes. It was like a blind being raised on a window, showing loss and anguish. 'Perhaps your mother . . .'

'My mother! She packed me off to boarding-school, then went overseas and stayed there.' Sophie could have wept hearing his words. He recovered quickly. 'We have an excellent relationship.' His smile was flippant, jarring. 'She never wants to see me, and I don't want to see her.'

Her heart in strips for him, she tried to understand. 'I can't condone your mother's action. Maybe she couldn't face you because that meant facing up to losing your brother and her husband.' She paused. 'Jon, I think you should write to her. She needs help as much as you. When you ran across the road it was the action of a thoughtless child. You have to forgive yourself . . .'

'Come off it!' His voice grated.

For several moments there was silence. Sophie could not tell his thoughts. He seemed to have shut himself away, and she had not the knowledge or skill to help him. For his sake, she risked his anger and spoke carefully.

'Until you come to terms with the past, I don't think you'll ever be a mature man, able to give love and receive it.'

He looked at her and shook his head. 'I've never heard such sentimental slobber!' He said the words with laughing cynicism, but Sophie knew the steel safe had been slammed on his past. She could not bring herself to look at him, so she hid her feelings by looking out of the window. The darkness seemed a portent.

'You're still a romantic, Sophie. I'm a realist. Romantics get crushed. You didn't learn the right lesson from your experience with Pierre. I'm a harder teacher. I want you to have no pretty fantasies about me, no illusions of a knight in shining armour.' His warning hurt her more. 'We've talked enough. Shall we go?'

The arrival of the proprietor to take the credit card was almost a relief. As he thanked the man, Jon appeared to be his charming, urbane self.

Outside, the cold air made her shiver despite her warm dress. Jon put an arm around her and she breathed a sigh of relief, thinking it was his way of acknowledging that she had only meant to help.

When he drew her closer she did not protest, choosing instead to divert him while she kept her own space. Hadn't he warned her to guard her feelings?

'There's still the snow wind biting. Look at the magnificence of the mountains in the moonlight.'

'Now who's playing tactics?' His eyes gleamed. 'We're lucky. A full moon. Isn't that for romantics?'

They had reached the car door so she merely smiled and waited as he reached past her with the key, his breath warm on the back of her neck. He finished unlocking the door, but paused before opening it. His hands went to her waist, holding her firmly while his mouth wrecked havoc with her emotions as he kissed her nape and her right ear.

'My sweet, skin-scented Sophie,' he murmured. 'I'm sorry. I know I hurt you. Sometimes I'm a scratchy old dog.'

Generous-hearted, she turned, instantly forgiving and understanding, raising her mouth for his kiss. She was aware of her body softening, arching against his and the passionate response. His mouth gentled her, his breath and his firm strong hands exciting her senses. Of their own volition her arms had curved round him, raising his shirt, her fingers seeking to know, gently probing and delighting in every small hollow, line and muscle of his chest, shoulders, neck and head. She answered his kiss totally, unable and unwilling to stop the avalanche of sensations which covered her, smothering her doubts and exposing only their need for each other.

'Sophie!'

As Jon said it her name was a song, his lips touching hers, his breath a caress. He released her slowly with tender reluctance. 'Patience, my sweet, sexy woman.'

He opened the car door and somehow she managed to sit down and fasten her seat-belt. She leant back, her scattered emotions gradually returning, only to eddy like dry leaves when Jon brushed a kiss against her cheek. As they drove she had time to recover, and then time to realise Jon had not taken advantage of her swiftly aroused passion to suggest a brief encounter in a hotel room. The new knowledge that she could trust Jon was like a light of happiness switched on in a dark room. She glowed softly with the thought that Jon had considered her, had understood and cared about her above his own desires.

He wasn't the womaniser she had despised when she had first read about him. He wasn't the tin man without a heart. Despite the tragedy in his life, he was a man who could love and she was a woman who wanted to love him!

Seeing him in the flickering pattern of the street lights, his face alternately highlighted and shadowed, gave her pleasure. Quietly watching him, his aggression masked by his relaxation and complete control, she knew he would not be an easy man to love. At the junction he stopped to allow a solitary car to pass and he glanced at her, his mouth curving, aware of her scrutiny.

'Do I pass?'

Her new knowledge was too delicate to risk his cynicism. 'You're very good-looking,' she prevaricated.

'So I've been told.'

'You've got an obstinate chin.'

'Me?'

Sophie laughed. 'Look in the mirror when you're shaving some time! Don't worry. You've the most delicious mouth.'

'All the better to kiss you with . . .' He turned the car and Sophie looked at him with more delight, realising he had taken the wrong way. To think that Jon with all his abilities was a bad navigator seemed to make him more lovable.

'Jon, you should have headed west there.' Her voice was husky with love. Unfazed, he slowed the car but continued to drive along the outlying street until he came to one of the few driveways. Instead of reversing, he drove in and halted the car at the rear of a small cottage.

'I seldom make a wrong turning, my sweet Sophie.' He bent and kissed her briefly, then undid her seat-belt. 'Surprise!' His eyes reflected his excitement as he gestured towards the house. Wondering who was expecting him, Sophie obediently followed him as he bounded forward to the well-lit entry. By the time she reached him the door was open. The faint, distinctive smell of new paint, wallpaper and carpet lingered.

'Come on in,' Jon commanded.

As she walked inside he touched a switch panel and she heard the click, then soft music began to surround them. Jon put one arm around her, guiding her into a large, well-proportioned living-room. Wide-eyed, she could only look at him, puzzled by the bareness of the hallway and living-room: no curtains, cushions, pictures or ornaments softening the hard outlines of its new ivory wallpaper and deep ruby carpet. An ivory leather suite looked as if the salesman had parked it there temporarily. She looked at Jon for clarification.

'Relax, Sophie. We're not intruding. I negotiated for this place a few days after I bought the lodge.' He smiled faintly and ran his fingers gently down the curve of her hairline and around her ear with devastating effect. She gasped and he kissed her thoroughly until she was fluid with desire. It took all her control to push him away in an attempt to remain sensible.

'But why?' she managed.

'Because you're a woman and I'm a man, my sweet, sexy blonde.'

He dropped a kiss, stopping her indignant protest. 'Oh, you mean the house?' His grin disarmed her. 'I decided I needed a base here and I had my agent scout around for one suitable. I was wanting something modern and practical, but he couldn't get one with the grounds big enough for a helicopter hangar. In sheer desperation, after I'd fired a few angry salvoes, he produced this place. As soon as I saw it, I bought it.' His hand took hers. 'It reminded me of you, Sophie. Small, elegant and stylish. Very private and rather old-fashioned.' His expression was tender but his voice was whimsical. 'Of course, I'm a twentieth-century man so there had to be a few changes inside, but I told my experts I wanted the character maintained. I'm very pleased with it.'

Sophie looked around her, wide-eyed, as he pointed out details.

'This was the front entrance and two rather poky living-rooms. I wanted the entrance to be at the rear, so we knocked out the side wall and put in a partition for the hall.' He looked as smug as if he had done the work himself, but Sophie, studying the room, could understand his pleasure.

'Result, you've a neat entry and one very pleasant room! The sun would be able to come in all day. Oh Jon, it's lovely. I can just see it with rather charming Victorian-style curtains, you know those . . . She broke off, aware of his smile. 'Have I said something wrong?'

'No, Sophie. I wanted you to do the interior, that's why I had it left at this stage. I spent more time dithering over whether you'd like carpet or Persian rugs than I would spend on checking the décor for an entire hotel.' His tone was rueful. 'And then I had to pick the colour. What do you think? It's not too dramatic?'

'It's perfect. You could always put a rug on top as a feature. I like the shade of ivory you've chosen for the walls and ceilings. It's warmer than white, yet lets in a lot of light.'

Jon smiled. 'Arctic blonde, like your hair!'

The kitchen made Sophie gasp with surprise. The cupboards hid all modern labour-saving devices, yet the joinery had been made from rimu and the pattern was similar to the details carved into the wood at Tiromaugna.

'But how?' Helplessly she looked at Jon.

'With money, it's possible to have specific designs made to suit. I wanted you to feel at home here.'

The bubble of happiness grew as she pondered his words. Jon led her along the passage to another door. 'This, you're going to love,' he promised as he opened it to reveal a large bedroom, again almost empty except for an ivory-coloured waterbed. Along one side a specialised trolley contained a monitor, keyboard and computer. Beyond it was an almost empty dressing-room and bathroom, but Sophie barely glanced at either, her eyes drawn to the wall of glass and its forest of plants.

'A conservatory!'

'Actually I insisted on a spa pool as one of my specific requirements. My architect looked at the difficulties, used his imagination and came up with this idea. The loss of the second bedroom is more than compensated for by having a spa in my own patch of jungle. From here and from outside it just looks like a Victorian conservatory, so again it blends with the original period.'

Sophie could only look in admiration as he led her into the jungle. It took some time to see the cunningly hidden climbing-frames and the irrigation outlets permanently hooked into place. The pool was the *pièce de résistance*. Twice the size of a normal spa, it glistened blue and inviting. He bent and scooped up some water, but pulled a face.

'Freezing!' he announced regretfully. 'There must be a bug in the house computer system. I inserted the codes to fill and heat the pool this morning, but it hasn't worked.'

He led the way back to the bedroom and sat down on the bed, pulling the computer trolley towards him with one hand, while with the other he undid and pulled off his tie. With the contented sigh of a man who was at ease, he kicked off his shoes.

'The computer here is one of my latest toys, a specialised one with programming for the house. I can arrange lighting, fill the spa and so forth by sending it a message from any one of my other offices.' He flicked a small button on the monitor and it lit. 'Well, what do you think?'

'I'm—I'm—I'm flabbergasted!'

He grinned happily. 'I just want a minute to reset

the heat on the spa control. OK? Take a seat.'

There were no chairs so she sat beside him, trying to appear serene and not uncomfortable about being on his bed. As he removed a floppy disk from the computer and inserted another, she reflected that she had no need for caution, as he was totally engrossed by the information appearing on the screen. His fingers flicked lightly over the keyboard with long familiarity, and his eyes scanned the monitor.

'I suppose I took it for granted you'd stay at the west wing or at the lodge itself,' she commented as he removed the second disk and replaced it. Another quick play on the keyboard and the screen graphed a spa pool and round-faced, happy bubbles with steam. Sophie saw a red light shine above the spa doorway. Satisfied, Jon adjusted the set and switched off the monitor.

'That's it,' he smiled. 'The resort is going to require a great deal of my personal involvement. Once it's established and operating smoothly, I'll extend my interests in the South Island. This place is handy to the local airfield. I can use the chopper and Highway One is only a few minutes away, plus it's close to Tiromaunga.'

He tugged off his jacket, threw it towards the end of the bed and pulled her close. His mouth teased hers into response.

'Mmm, that's better,' he murmured. 'You're the main reason I couldn't stay here. Too distracting.' His eyes were more blue than ever. 'With the reactions we had each time we met, I knew we would be lovers or enemies. Either way, a house was necessary.'

Sophie drew away, but Jon tightened his arms and lay back, pulling her with him. His kiss seared her, as though daring her to deny the willingness of her body.

'Don't be a contumacious female,' he muttered. 'You want me as much as I want you.' His hands slid over her body possessively until they rested on her neat buttocks, effectively locking her hips against his. Ignoring her protests, his kiss plundered her emotions until he released her. 'We're not exactly a pair of spotty teenagers, Sophie.'

'So you shouldn't behave like a grasping, grubby street kid,' she shot, her breathing ragged. 'I'm not some prize you have to pinch.'

His surprise was obvious, but he was fast with his recovery.

'Don't come the outraged snow queen! A few minutes ago you were seducing me. Remember?'

Sophie sat up slowly. The pain in her body showed in her eyes. 'You said we'd be lovers or enemies. But you've said nothing about love,' she said simply.

CHAPTER NINE

'LOVE?' Jon's scorn was acid. 'Love is a temporary emotion which makes fools of all concerned. I told you, I'm a realist. As far as I'm concerned our relationship would be based on mutual physical satisfaction. We play the game as adults, the rules being to take the necessary precautions.'

'And the time? Is it a one-night or several-night stand?' She hardly recognised her own voice, thick with hurt.

'One-night stands are not my scene.' It was his turn to sound outraged. 'In the hotel game you learn fast. They can be deadly, and I'm not that stupid.' He plucked out a couple of clips so his fingers could ruffle through her hair. When he spoke again his tone was gentle, conciliatory. 'Sophie, I bought this house for us. It's a long time since I was interested in a semi-permanent relationship with a woman, but since I met you I've hardly had you out of my mind. I can tell from your hunger when we kiss that it's the same for you. We're very, very lucky.'

As though to prove his point he began kissing her, dotting her face, her nape, her ears erotically with his mouth until her feelings swirled. She made a panic-stricken protest and he held her, instantly reassuring.

'With both of us understanding the rules, you won't get hurt, Sophie. When I'm based here I'd like you to be available for me at certain times. We can discuss that later. I'll endeavour to arrange my business to give you as much of my time as possible. There will be times when you may like to join me elsewhere. That choice is entirely yours.'

'With the proviso that business comes first?' She was staggered by his proposal. He gentled her shoulder, then began stroking her neck and back with long, sensuous, slow movements.

'Sophie, I can feel your anger. I'm sorry. It sounds selfish, but there is no other way. I am responsible for the temporary well-being of several hundred travellers and the good employment of many staff. I have directorships in two large companies as well as being chairman of my own major holding investment company. People have trusted me with their money.'

'Money?'

She sat up, disgusted. He misinterpreted her.

'Good point. I'd almost forgotten it. See the effect you have on me?' He began unbuttoning his shirt. 'All arranged. As of now you're employed on my personal staff under the title of caretaker here. You'll receive a generous wage and an expense account for the house. Also, if there is any special little thing you'd like, just ask. I won't be Santa Claus, but I'm not Scrooge either. I'll leave you my private box number so you can have the decorating accounts forwarded. You'll be able to communicate with me either through the computer or the telephone.

He reached for his jacket and pulled out a flat jewellery box.

'A small token. Diamonds are a girl's best friend and all that.' He took her wrist and fastened on the gold and diamond studded bracelet while she watched frozenly. 'It's a little large, but I can have that adjusted.' He checked the catch again and glanced at her, but her eyes were riveted by the glittering gift. 'First time I've known you short of words, Sophie.'

He stood up and moved across to the dressing-room. 'I think we've covered everything.' She could see him mentally going through the different points. 'Not exactly the right choice of phrase,' he added as he pulled his shirt off.

Sophie was so stunned, she remained on the bed. Her thoughts of love and trust were puffs in the wind. He cared nothing for her except as an attractive doll he was prepared to buy. The glittering bracelet felt like a band of white fire around her heart. Tugging at it, she pulled it off still fastened and threw it on to the computer. Removing the bracelet freed her from the frozen stupor. Shock, hurt and anger clawed her into action. She wanted to run, to flee, to hide, but her burning anger would not allow her such an easy course. Before she left she would tell him exactly what she thought of his arrogance and what he could do with his offer!

She stood up and the waterbed moved. The thought of pulling the plug on it was tempting, but not deflating enough. He needed a bucket of cold water tipped over him, but buckets were in short

supply, although there was cold water in the spa.
Her eyes sparkled at the thought of throwing Jon
into the pool. Logic told her that as he was so much
larger and superbly fit there was little possibility of
achieving such action. Unless she could catch him
off balance. But how could she do that?

Inspired, her eyes went to the diamond bracelet
and she snatched it back. With a savage smile she
ran to the spa and studied its shape and steps.
Rapidly she decided that if she could drop the
bracelet on the second step in the water, beyond her
reach, but within stretch by Jon, he would lean over
to retrieve it. And if at that moment she gave him a
swift push, surely he would crash into the pool? The
picture produced was pleasurable.

Sitting down on the lowest dry step, she carefully
dropped the offensive gift into the freezing water.
She had underestimated the slight movement of the
water, and the bracelet dropped to the edge of the
second step, hung tantalisingly, then fell to the base.
Her involuntary cry of dismay was genuine.

'Jon!'

His arrival was swift. 'Something wrong?'

Hastily she turned back to the spa.

'Your bracelet.' She pointed down to the floor of
the pool. She heard him mutter an expletive. Not
daring to raise her head she saw his feet walk round
the perimeter of the pool until they halted beside
her.

'Leave it. In the morning the pool will be warm
and we can go fishing. Could even be fun.'

She hadn't thought of such a logical response, and

she stiffened as he lowered himself to sit beside her. Her plan was going badly wrong.

'You look a little overdressed for bed, Sophie. Shall I help?'

He lifted off her gold chain and placed it over a plant. She was fuming when he bent, turned her head round and kissed her very deliberately. The taste of toothpaste and the tang of his special cologne mixed with his own warm, male scent sent a rush of sensuality through her, but she pulled back.

'No!'

'Sophie, you're not going to insist on wearing the wretched bracelet right now, are you?'

'It might get lost. Your computer might empty the pool,' she babbled. 'After all, it did have one problem before. Somebody might accidentally tap in the codes.'

'The computer is on house control, so that won't happen. Relax, Sophie.'

'Your arms are quite long; if you stretched you might reach it.'

'They're not made of elastic.'

As though to convince her of that, he shot one arm out and caught her close while the other tipped her head so she had to face him and his lips touched her mouth. She pushed her lips together tightly to block his kiss.

'Why are you giving me the cabbage patch doll act?' He released her abruptly. 'That blasted bracelet!' He stood up. 'I suppose I could use one of the stakes from the plants.'

Bending over the pool to check the depth, he

presented a perfect target. Sophie acted. The splash as he fell into the water was sweet music. She laughed as she brushed away some of the drops which had reached her, while he surfaced, spluttering and streaming. It was a moment she would never forget, decided Sophie, as she enjoyed her revenge.

'You did that deliberately, you little monster!' He wiped the wet hair back from his face to clear her vision.

'Yes.'

Irate, he began to climb from the spa. Sophie's mirth changed to a shriek when he picked her up, held her high and carried her out to the middle of the pool. He stopped and, still holding her inches about the water, spoke softly. 'Sophie, did that bracelet fall in accidentally?'

'No.'

The cold water hit her as he opened his arms and she fell into the pool. Gasping with the shock, she righted herself and swam to the side. It was her turn to struggle out, wet and bedraggled, while he smiled.

'Perhaps you could fetch your bracelet while you're there.'

'Keep your gifts,' she stormed. 'Look at me.'

'Highly diverting, but you know what cold water does,' he shot as he walked to a side door which opened to the bathroom. 'You can share a hot shower with me, or else wait!'

She heard the shower run and saw the clouds of steam while she stood shivering. The prospect of dry towels lured her into the bathroom. Having found some, she pulled off her heavy, wet dress and searched in the adjoining dressing-room for something to wear.

'It's all yours, Sophie.' He entered the room with a large towel wrapped round his waist.

'I want your assurance that you won't invade my privacy.' She spoke firmly, despite the tremors that gripped her.

'Go ahead. You're safe. You look about as attractive as a frog at this moment.'

Dignity and cold combined to hold her head high as she moved past him. The shower was blissfully warm, restoring her to normal temperature. She dried herself off and pulled on the shirt and dressing gown she had found. Back in the dressing-room hairdryer placed ready for her was a peace offer Finished, she wrapped her wet gear up in a t and carried it out to the kitchen where Jon w preparing some coffee. He poured in a tot of Irish whiskey then opened a packet of long-life cream.

'Dump your wet stuff on the bench and come through.' He carried the coffee-mugs leading the way to the couch in the living-room. Deliberately she chose one of the single chairs. He handed her the coffee and took the couch, lounging on it casually. It was only then that she realised he was fully dressed.

'I'll drive you back to Tiromaunga when you've finished your coffee, Sophie.'

'Thank you.'

She tried her coffee but it was too hot to do more than sip at. They might have been two strangers,

Sophie thought miserably. She tried to summon her anger, but she could find none.

'So tell me what I did wrong?' Jon looked at her. 'I thought I'd set everything up right. I've never wanted anyone as much as I wanted to make love to you tonight.'

'Jon, it wouldn't have been making love. You wanted sex with me. That's all it would have meant to you. I was someone you could prostitute.'

'Others would have been glad enough.'

'But you didn't choose them, you wanted me,' she reminded him. The distance between them seemed too great. She put down her mug and crossed to sit on the floor in front of him, facing him directly, ⬛ddenly fighting for his understanding.

⬛ on! You said this house reminded you of me, ⬛ll and old-fashioned. You remade it to match ⬛r life-style, but you did it with care, with love for ⬛s special character, its integrity. If I change my values to fit your needs, then I alter my character, my integrity. I love you too much for that.'

The truth surprised both of them.

Unable to say more, Sophie dropped her eyelids, bending her head to her hands, already knowing his denial, but praying for a miracle.

It seemed a long, agonising time before he spoke. 'I can't tell you pretty lies, Sophie. I can't say "I love you". It's not an emotion I feel.' He waited until she looked at him. 'I can say I want you and mean it. I can tell you that I find you beautiful and mean it. But don't expect me to say "I love you". I'm not a hypocrite.'

There were tears wobbling in her eyes as she nodded understanding.

Jon stood up urgently. 'Let's go.'

The trip west was quiet, the moonlit mountain-tops a frieze in the sky. Each was busy with their own thoughts. It was only as Jon turned the car into the tree-lined drive of Tiromaunga that she remembered her damp bundle of clothes.

'Jon, I'm sorry, I left my stuff in a towel. Also Dad's gold chain!'

'I'll give you a spare key. It was cut for you, in any case.' He rolled the car to a quiet stop beside the house. On the key-ring he selected a key and twisted it off. 'Goodnight, Sophie. I'll see you in a month.' He tried to lighten their mood. 'Maybe next time you'll join me in a hot spa.'

'I'll keep my pink dress specially for it,' she promised with a brave smile. It faltered as he drew her back towards him, and his mouth touched hers with such tenderness that she wanted to cry. 'Take care of yourself, Jonathon Roberts.'

'I have to, don't I? My caretaker isn't going to be with me.'

Unable to hold back her emotions any longer, she left him and ran to the welcoming wings of the homestead, which seemed like arms reassuring her of security and love. She slipped her key into the lock and reset the alarm. Outside, the car's engine spun into action. Tiptoeing quietly along the passage, she jumped guiltily when the grandfather clock struck the hour, and she entered her bedroom, glad her father had gone to bed. Her appearance in Jon's shirt and dressing-gown would have been hard to explain.

In the morning, Sophie drove back to the cottage. In daylight she could appreciate the simplicity and strength of the colonial structure, much about it reminding her of Tiromaunga. Only the wide expanse of rear lawn with its marked circle and the new hangar and garage hinted at the changes. A century-old walnut tree stood like a guardian in the far corner, and she guessed that at one stage the lawn would have been a family's vegetable garden. She slipped the key into the lock and pushed open the door.

'Good morning, Sophie.'

She spun round at Jon's voice.

'Relax, Sophie. This is a recording, so regrettably I can't make attacks on your virtue. At the moment you're quite safe. You will recall discussing decorating this house last night. I'd like you to complete furnishing it for me. Your fees would be paid at the standard rate and any accounts you could hand to my staff at the lodge.'

There was a long pause, and Sophie mentally debated whether she should accept the proposal.

'Sophie, you'll find the plans in the study. I've put them in the second drawer of the desk.' A touch of humour shaded his voice. 'By the way, if you feel like a hot spa, go ahead. It will empty automatically tonight. I have to leave now, Sophie. Over to you.'

The small click told her the tape had switched

itself off. The house seemed warm and friendly with the sunshine glowing through the uncurtained windows. She wandered from room to room, loving the cottage, but disturbed when reminders of Jon kept intruding, like the faint tang of his cologne lingering in the air.

Although she needed work and she yearned to decorate the cottage, the knowledge of having to think constantly about Jon's likes and dislikes deterred her. Having made up her mind, she entered the conservatory to retrieve her gold chain. It lay looped over a plant where Jon had wound it, and as she held it in her fingers she realised how fortunate her own past had been. What effects would such a tragedy as Jon had experienced have had on her?

She had always known love as constant until Pierre had made a mockery of it. The experience had scarred her, destroying her faith in her own ability to accept love. It had been the gentle love of her father and their friends which had gradually restored her, and Jon's shocking tactics had opened her to emotions again. Had Jon reacted in a similar way after his tragedy? Unable to trust love, had he knotted his own safety net and refused to allow his emotions out? How much of his constant search for a challenge was caused by his inability to love?

Thoughtfully she sat by the steps, looking at the water. Wasn't Jon's offer more honest than Pierre's protestations of love? Hadn't Jon deliberately set out the parameters of his offer so she knew love did not enter into the relationship? It was to be like a business contract, something he could trust. He would never understand her feelings until he was able to love. The knowledge made her feel sad.

Idly, she flicked the water and felt its warmth on her hand. The spa looked so tempting that she decided it was one invitation she could accept from Jon. Removing her clothes took seconds, and as she entered the water the spa automatically turned on. It felt wonderfully relaxing, gently bubbling away the tensions and stresses and doubts. She wished there was some way she could love Jon without denying her own self. Lying in the pool, she sat up suddenly with the simplicity of the answer.

She would decorate his cottage and she would make it so beautiful that love would shine through through it like the sunlight, not only the interior, but also in the forgotten garden. Enthralled by the possibility, she stopped soaking, realising that she had a lot to do. Hauling herself out of the spa, she dressed and again walked slowly through the house, checking the view from each window, planning the garden spots from the inside angles as well as outside. It was some time before she was ready to leave, the house plans clutched firmly in one hand and the damp, soggy bundle of clothes and towels in the other.

Back at Tiromaunga, she spread the plans out over the large dining-table, so it wasn't long before they caught her father's attention.

'Where did you get hold of these, Sophie?'

'They belong to Jon. It's a place he's bought as a base. He wants me to decorate it for him. It's just a small cottage, probably earlier than Tiromaunga, but I felt at home there.'

'Hardly surprising; look at the original architect.' Her father's fingers pointed to the corner inscription. 'He's the same! And there's the date, ten years earlier than the start of Tiromaunga.'

'No wonder I loved it! I'm longing to go to the Canterbury Museum and check out the designs available then. Hopefully I might see something in the similar mood and design in the furnishing shops. I thought I might make some patchwork . . .'

'I hope you know what you've let yourself in for!'

'Dad, when you see the place you'll understand. Everything has to be perfect.'

'I gather the evening went well last night.'

'Let's just say it didn't turn out the way either of us hoped, but I think we each learnt something. Jon has a tragic past and I think it explains a lot about him.'

'So long as you don't get hurt, Sophie.'

'Who, me?' She didn't want to talk about her relationship with Jon. 'Dad, would you mind calling out the window measurements while I write them down?' It was a diversionary tactic worthy of Jon, she reflected wryly. 'At the moment the curtains are my first priority. I'll ring through an order for the linings so they can be made up. The faster the carpet is protected, the better, and it might take ages before I can find the right furnishing fabric. This is going to be fun, Dad—and to think I'm being paid for it, too!'

By dinner-time Sophie had checked off a list covering everything from pictures to light fittings. As she made a note of possible shops the telephone rang, disrupting her carefully piled notes.

'Sophie?' His voice was deep and warm.

'Jon! You now have a decorator for the cottage. I heard your message.' She felt ridiculously light-hearted just to know he had rung.

'You'll do it? That's the best news I've heard all day.'

'I've rung through an order for the linings, and tomorrow I intend going to Christchurch to have a look round. I may stay overnight.'

'I have a better idea. Fly up here for a couple of days. There's a flight leaving Christchurch in an hour and a half. Be on it, Sophie. I'll fly the chopper to meet you at the airport myself.' His voice quietened and became deeper. 'Come and stay with me, sweet Sophie. I'd start by kissing you, then I'd undress you very slowly so I could see you. I want to know and touch every part of your beautiful body.'

Sophie felt her bones turn liquid at the sensuous tones. She sat down hastily, struggling with her own desires, but aware that he did not consider her share in their lovemaking . . .

'It's no use, Jon. Nothing's changed since last night.' She waited for him to suggest otherwise, but he was silent. 'Jon, I'll say goodbye.'

Replacing the receiver, she sat back in the chair,

her feelings an ocean of misery the size of the Pacific. Her earlier happiness in planning the details of the house as a way of giving her love seemed pathetic. For several moments she wondered if she should tell Jon she had changed her mind about decorating the cottage, but the work sheets drew her back. She wanted it to be beautiful.

Over the following month she worked consistently at the cottage or in its garden. She cleared two semicircular areas against the fence, dug and mulched them, then laid heavy plastic and covered it with a layer of bark. Slitting holes, she carefully transplanted ruby granny bonnets, blue delphiniums and ruby and pink dahlias. Among the trees she planted several old climbing roses, and at their base she set ruby-coloured fuchsias where they would provide a splash of colour.

On wet days and in her spare time she busied herself with her patchwork, threading in colours to match the furnishing fabric. Her hunt for curtains had been so successful, she had scarcely been able to credit her good fortune. The Victorian-replica design with its cream background and highly colourful ruby, blue, navy and green flowers and birds fitted with the carpet exactly. An antiques shop had been her source of supply for two hanging lamps for the main living-room, and she could only hope another dealer would provide her with more for the hallway. Some pieces of ruby glass she had collected while hunting for lights formed a splash of colour.

For the bedroom she had been delighted with a

table lamp and a ceiling light which pictured old red roses. On the bed lay the jewel-coloured patch-work duvet cover she had made. The little clock Jon had given her sat by the computer desk. Looking round, Sophie was pleased with her efforts. The whole room seemed to dance, the net curtains filtering the sunlight and the heavy curtains pulled to the sides like a gay picture-frame for the view to the garden, linking it with the wall of plants in the conservatory.

It was ready for Jon's return, and although he had not bothered to inform her she knew he would arrive during the day. The clue had been the filling of the spa pool and the fact that the heaters and vents were switched on when she had arrived. Mentally she had prepared herself, lecturing herself on the importance of keeping her feelings under firm control. She had already decided she would not allow Jon within arm's reach; she would be rational, cool and businesslike. Apart from the solitary telephone call when she had rejected his offer to fly north, she had not heard from him, and the long silence had convinced her he had taken her goodbye seriously. On pay days she had longed to ask the staff at the lodge about him, but her pride would not allow the questions.

The sound of a helicopter drew her to the window and she watched as it came closer. Her heart began beating faster and she grabbed her car keys, wanting to flee. The noise level as it began to descend told her it was too late. Hurriedly she combed her hair and checked her make-up, then, reminding herself to be the professional employee, she walked to the entry. The clatter of noise dropped to a faint drone then to silence, and she saw Jon slide open the door and jump out.

'Welcome home, Jon!' Her formal courtesy was mocked by the joy in her heart when she saw him. She could feel her resolution crumble as he looked at her, his smile lighting his blue eyes.

'You're right, Sophie. It feels as if I've come home.'

The tenderness in his eyes made her lock her suddenly weak knees together for support. She drew a quick breath and reminded herself she was not going to be his plaything. Hadn't he ignored her for a month? A whole thirty days and nights of anger and pain, of longing and frustration, little comfort in knowing her decision had been right. She tried to feel anger with him, but she was so pleased to see him she ached to throw her arms around him and kiss him. Her hands clenched into fists as she fought to maintain her composure.

'You've been busy.' He gestured to the garden. 'The place has found its dignity again.'

The compliment delighted her. 'It should be nearly maintenance-free, apart from the lawns.'

'I don't recall an account for the landscape gardener's services.'

'I didn't think it was necessary. I wanted to do it myself.'

It was an agony standing ramrod-stiff when she yearned to be beside him, proudly pointing out the features. As though he had read her thoughts, he took her arm.

'Later I hope you will show me round. Now I'd like you to show me the cottage.'

'Of course.' The words plopped out like unshed tears as she wondered how he could remain so detached, so unaffected by the bond of physical attraction which had flared when he took her hand. She removed it from his grip with the excuse of opening the door.

In the hallway he paused to look around, clearly pleased with the welcoming touches of the brass coat and umbrella stand and large brass urn containing flowers. A picture she had ordered to be framed, of the architect's original watercolour and ink sketch of the cottage, fitted neatly in pride of place.

'I noticed the sketch among the plans, but I didn't realise how good it would look framed.' Jon admired it closely. 'A rare treasure, Sophie.'

Together they made their way through the house, but Sophie excused herself when he entered the bedroom on the pretext of making a drink. Apart from his eyes smiling at her, he let her retreat pass without comment. She was shaking as she leant against the kitchen bench to fill the kettle. Jon's reactions to her work had been enthusiastic and appreciative, but she didn't know how much more of his charm she could take.

'Sophie, come here!'

Her fingers grew nerveless and she dropped the kettle in the sink, spilling the water.

'Leave it, my darling little stubborn Sophie.'

His voice was a sensuous murmur as he stood in the doorway. 'Come here and stop pretending you can't stand me. You love me. The whole place shouts it.'

'You can see that?'

He nodded and reached for her, drawing her forward the last few steps. She felt her skin tremble as he held her, and knew that he would have felt it, too.

'Please, Jon, let me go.' She was panting with emotion.

'No.'

She had forgotten how blue his eyes were, how the expression in them could be so tender. He bent and kissed her, his lips barely sweeping hers. All her determination slid off as she put her arms around him, full of love, aching for his touch. The gentleness when his mouth covered hers quickly changed to a deep, searching hunger, and her swift response aroused a passion that left her exposed, breathless and shaken.

'Sophie!' He said her name with tender triumph. 'Sophie, my very own woman.' He covered her face, her hair, her ears, her nape with a myriad kisses then his lips took hers again, setting waves of sensuous feelings crashing through her.

'It's . . . not . . . fair!' she protested weakly while her mouth still moved greedily for his kisses.

'All's fair in love and war, my darling Sophie.' His breath was a riot in her ear as his fingers traced curls of love in her hair. 'I love you, my sweet Sophie.'

His words, spoken softly as he held her firmly, were like a splash of cold water.

'What did you say?' She looked at him, devastated that he could descend to such dishonesty. White-faced and shocked, she pulled away.

'I love you, Sophie.'

'Don't say it, please. I can't bear it.'

'Sophie, I've spent this last month trying to live without you. It hasn't been easy. You kept interrupting me in the middle of dictating letters, smiling at me while I ate lunch and making love to me at night. Believe me, that's an exercise in frustration! My secretary told me I was in love and I fired her.' He smiled. 'Don't worry, she lives in the danger zone and thrives. As a matter of fact she had a copy of your picture framed for my desk. Naturally I shoved it in a drawer and got on with my work.'

'Naturally.' Sophie was beginning to feel flowers of joy growing.

'I kept thinking about things you said. I wrote to my mother. When I was finished in Australia I flew over to Edinburgh to see her. It was a pretty emotional time all round.'

'And . . .' She held her breath, but already knew the answer.

'Everything's fine.' He stopped and kissed her gently. 'Thanks to a certain strong-minded young woman who forced me to see another viewpoint.'

'Jon, I'm so pleased for you and your mother.' She sniffed back the quick emotion.

'My own sweet, sentimental Sophie.' He tightened his hold on her and kissed her. 'I spent a week with my family getting to know them. But you know what drove me home?'

'Business?'

'You, my darling Sophie. I'd convinced myself that given time you would fall like a plum into my hands. It wasn't until I was flying back that I began to realise I'd fallen in love with you. I told myself it was jet lag, and once I'd had a good sleep I'd be over it. That was a week ago.' He bent and kissed her briefly. 'I've been doing my inspections and driving myself hard to block out the thoughts of you. This morning my secretary said she couldn't take me any longer, handed me the plane tickets and ordered the chopper to be fuelled and on standby at Christchurch.

'I could hardly wait to hold you in my arms, and then I saw you looking so coolly serene and so unapproachable, I thought I'd lost you. But no woman would make a patchwork cover for a man's bed unless she loved him. And I love you, Sophie.'

The touch of his mouth seemed to sing its way triumphantly through her body, her own love responding instantly to him. When he released her she leant against him, her eyes smiling.

'And is it so bad to be in love with me?'

'No, it's right.' His voice was a deep, musical note in her ear. 'I knew that as soon as you kissed me.'

Sophie felt him hold her, cradling her so he could kiss her with slow tenderness.

'For us, Sophie, it has to be a total commitment. Sharing our bad times and our good times.'

She looked at him, loving him. Their kiss was a

silent vow.

'We can get married at Tiromaunga,' he continued. 'Where I first saw you. The trees will be our cathedral.'

'And what if it rains?' she teased.

'I couldn't care less if it snowed!' His eyes were blue sapphires. 'But don't worry, it won't. On you, the sun has to shine.'

And as usual he was right!

Six exciting series for you every month... from Harlequin

Harlequin Romance·
The series that started it all

Tender, captivating and heartwarming...
love stories that sweep you off to faraway places
and delight you with the magic of love.

◆

Harlequin Presents·
Powerful contemporary love stories...as individual as the women who read them

The No. 1 romance series...
exciting love stories for you, the woman of today...
a rare blend of passion and dramatic realism.

◆

Harlequin Superromance®
It's more than romance... it's Harlequin Superromance

A sophisticated, contemporary romance-fiction
series, providing you with a longer,
more involving read...a richer mix of complex plots
realism and adventure.

Harlequin
American Romance™
Harlequin celebrates the American woman...

...by offering you romance stories written about American women, by American women for American women. This series offers you contemporary romances uniquely North American in flavor and appeal.

◆

Harlequin Temptation
Passionate stories for today's woman

An exciting series of sensual, mature stories of love...dilemmas, choices, resolutions... all contemporary issues dealt with in a true-to-life fashion by some of your favorite authors.

◆

Harlequin Intrigue
Because romance can be quite an adventure

Harlequin Intrigue, an innovative series that blends the romance you expect... with the unexpected. Each story has an added element of intrigue that provides a new twist to the Harlequin tradition of romance excellence.

Harlequin Books

PROD-A-2